EDGAR ALLAN POE

Edgar Allan Poe Graphic Novels
are published by Stone Arch Books,
A Capstone Imprint, 1710 Roe Crest Drive
North Mankato, MN 56003
www.capstonepub.com

Cataloging-in-Publication Data is available on the Library of Congress website.

ISBN: 978-1-4342-3024-9 (library binding)
ISBN: 978-1-4342-4258-7 (paperback)
ISBN: 978-1-4342-5965-3 (eBook)

Summary: The Usher mansion is in shambles and slowly sinking into the marsh
below. Its inhabitants are sickly and slipping into madness. Voracious ivy
creeps over the house. The wind whispers eerie omens. And the trees creak
as their branches reach out to greet its newest visitor...

Art Director: Bob Lentz
Graphic Designer: Hilary Wacholz
Edited by: Sean Tulien

Printed in the United States of America in Stevens Point, Wisconsin.
072013   007593R

THE FALL OF THE HOUSE OF USHER

BY EDGAR ALLAN POE
RETOLD BY MATTHEW K. MANNING
ILLUSTRATED BY JIM JIMENZ

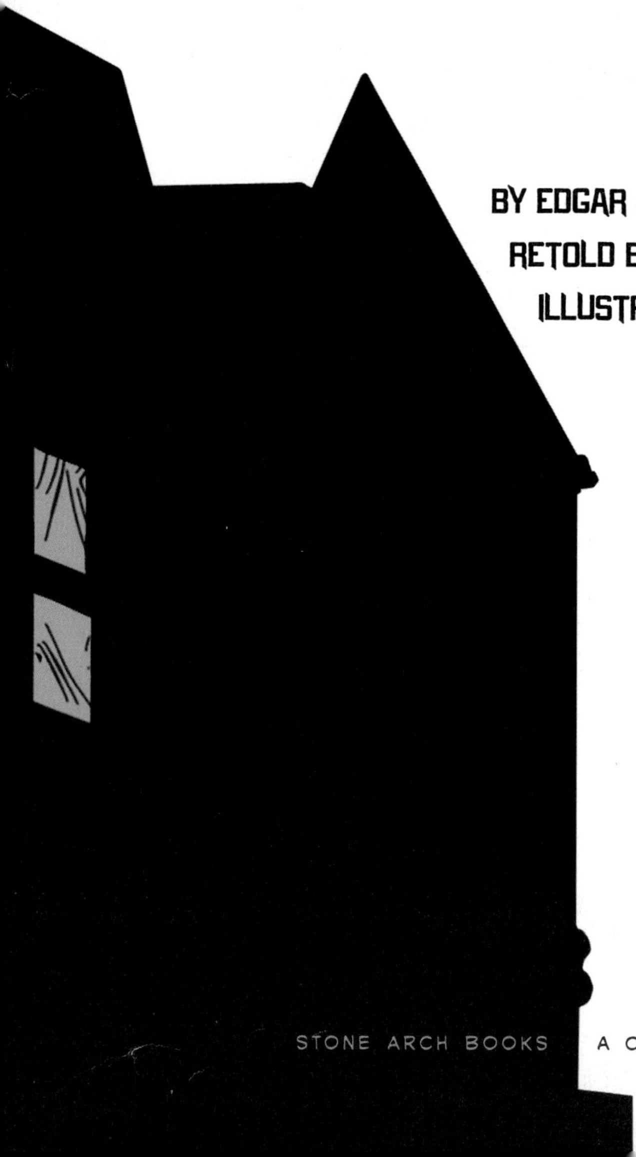

STONE ARCH BOOKS A CAPSTONE IMPRINT

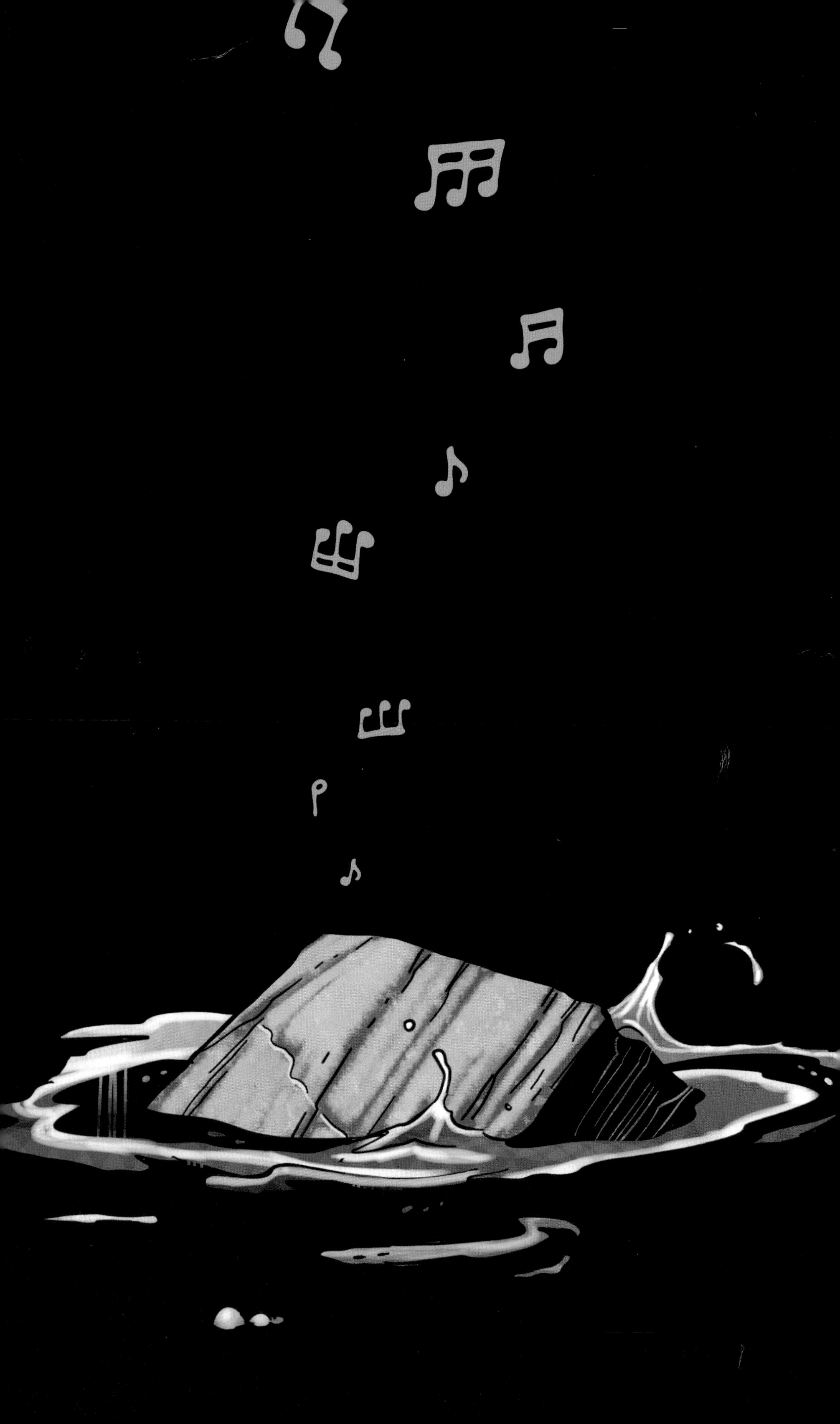

His heart is like a poised lute;
As soon as it is touched, it resounds.

— De Béranger

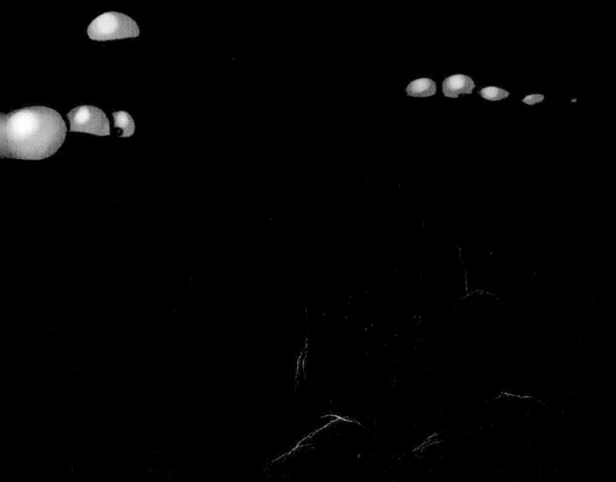

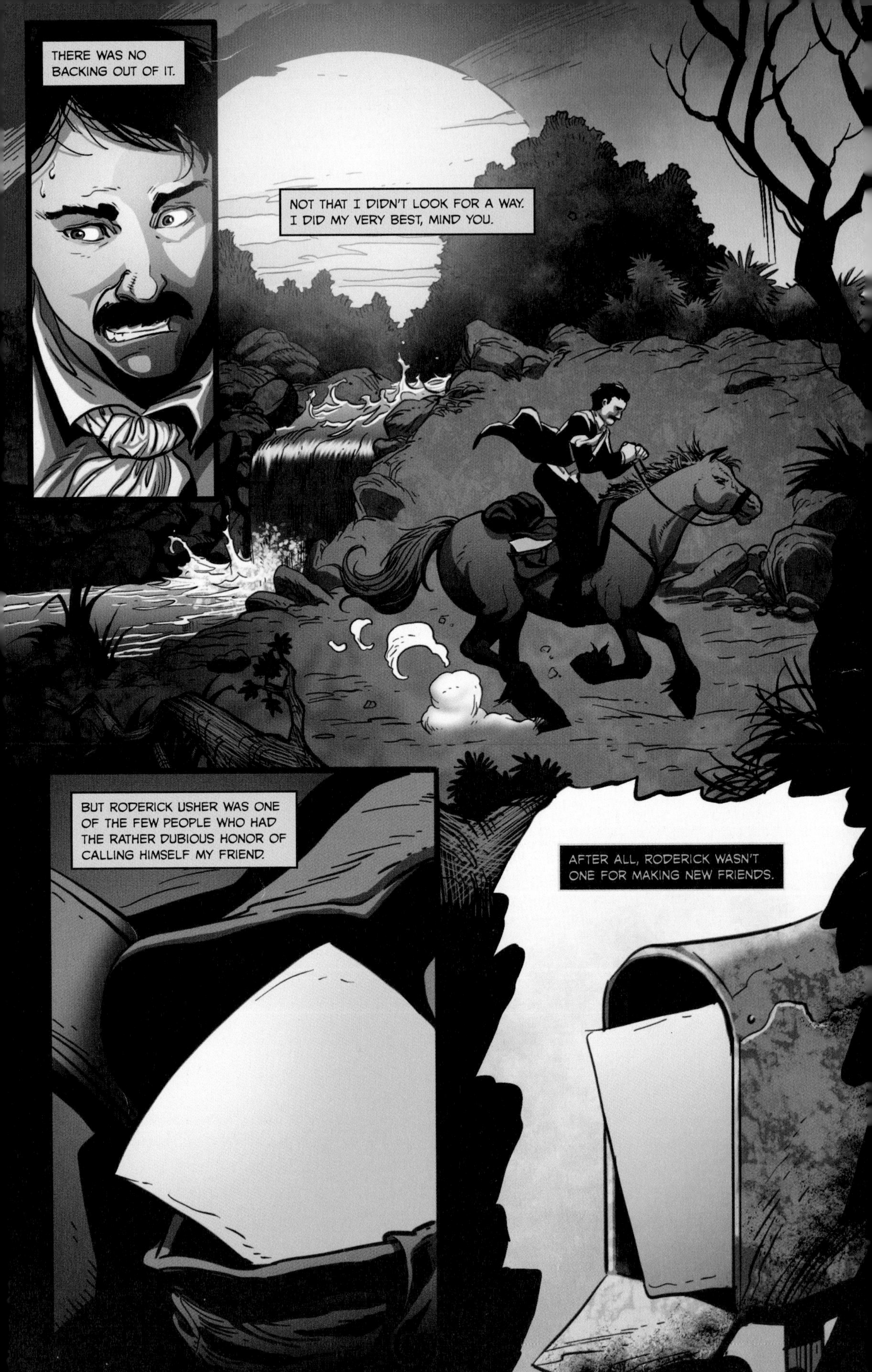
THERE WAS NO BACKING OUT OF IT.
NOT THAT I DIDN'T LOOK FOR A WAY. I DID MY VERY BEST, MIND YOU.
BUT RODERICK USHER WAS ONE OF THE FEW PEOPLE WHO HAD THE RATHER DUBIOUS HONOR OF CALLING HIMSELF MY FRIEND.
AFTER ALL, RODERICK WASN'T ONE FOR MAKING NEW FRIENDS.

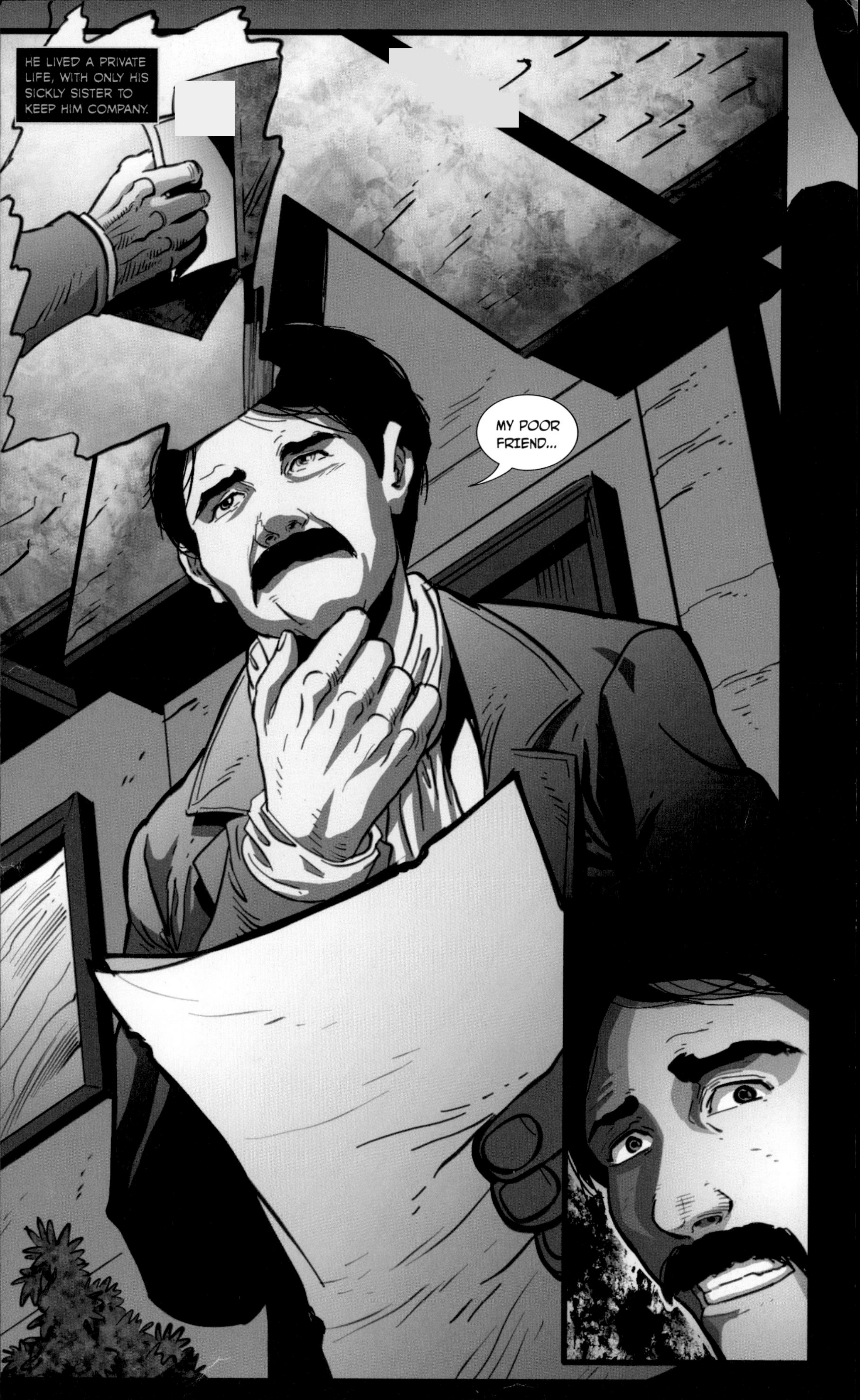
HE LIVED A PRIVATE LIFE, WITH ONLY HIS SICKLY SISTER TO KEEP HIM COMPANY.
MY POOR FRIEND...

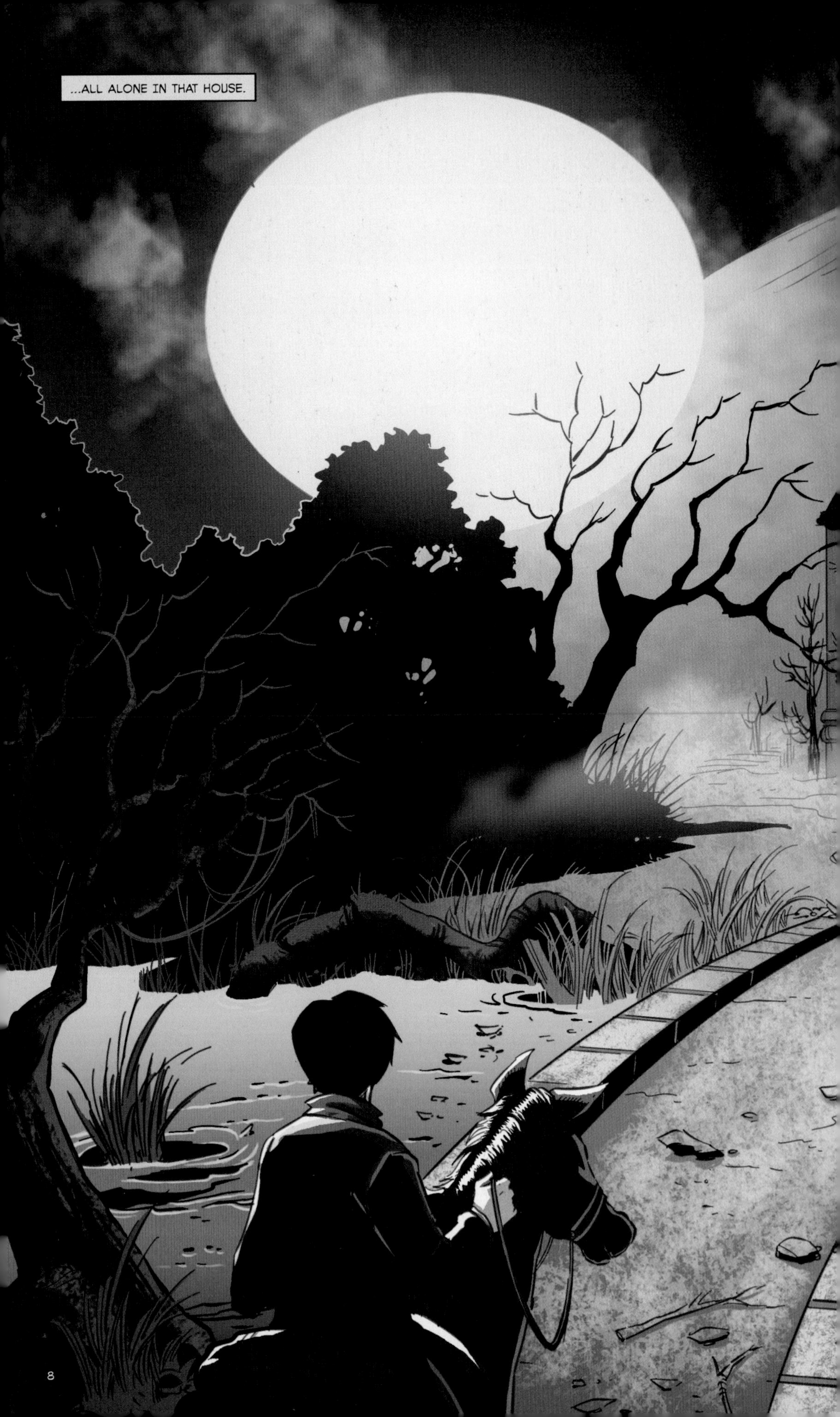
...ALL ALONE IN THAT HOUSE.

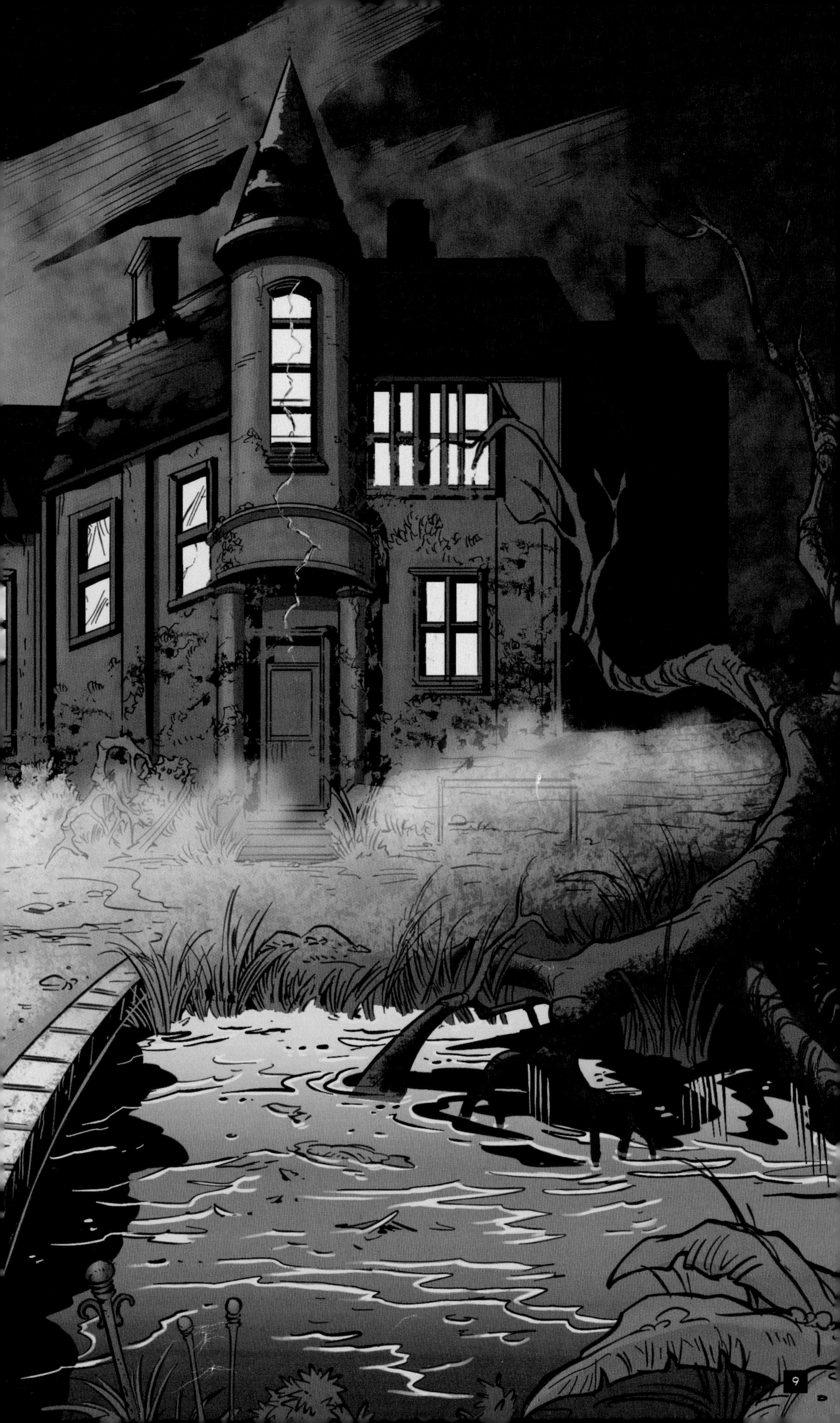

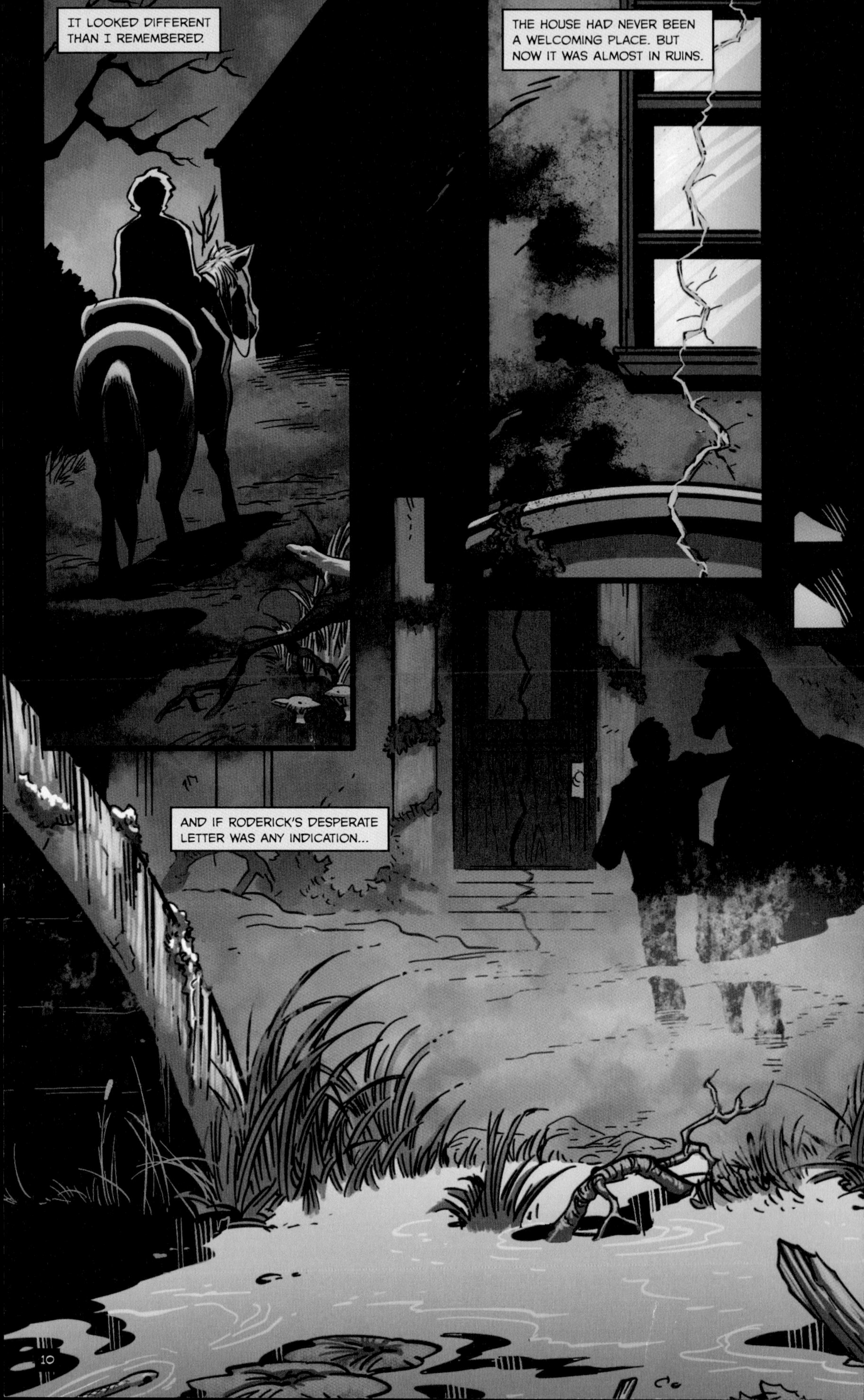
IT LOOKED DIFFERENT THAN I REMEMBERED.
THE HOUSE HAD NEVER BEEN A WELCOMING PLACE. BUT NOW IT WAS ALMOST IN RUINS.
AND IF RODERICK'S DESPERATE LETTER WAS ANY INDICATION...

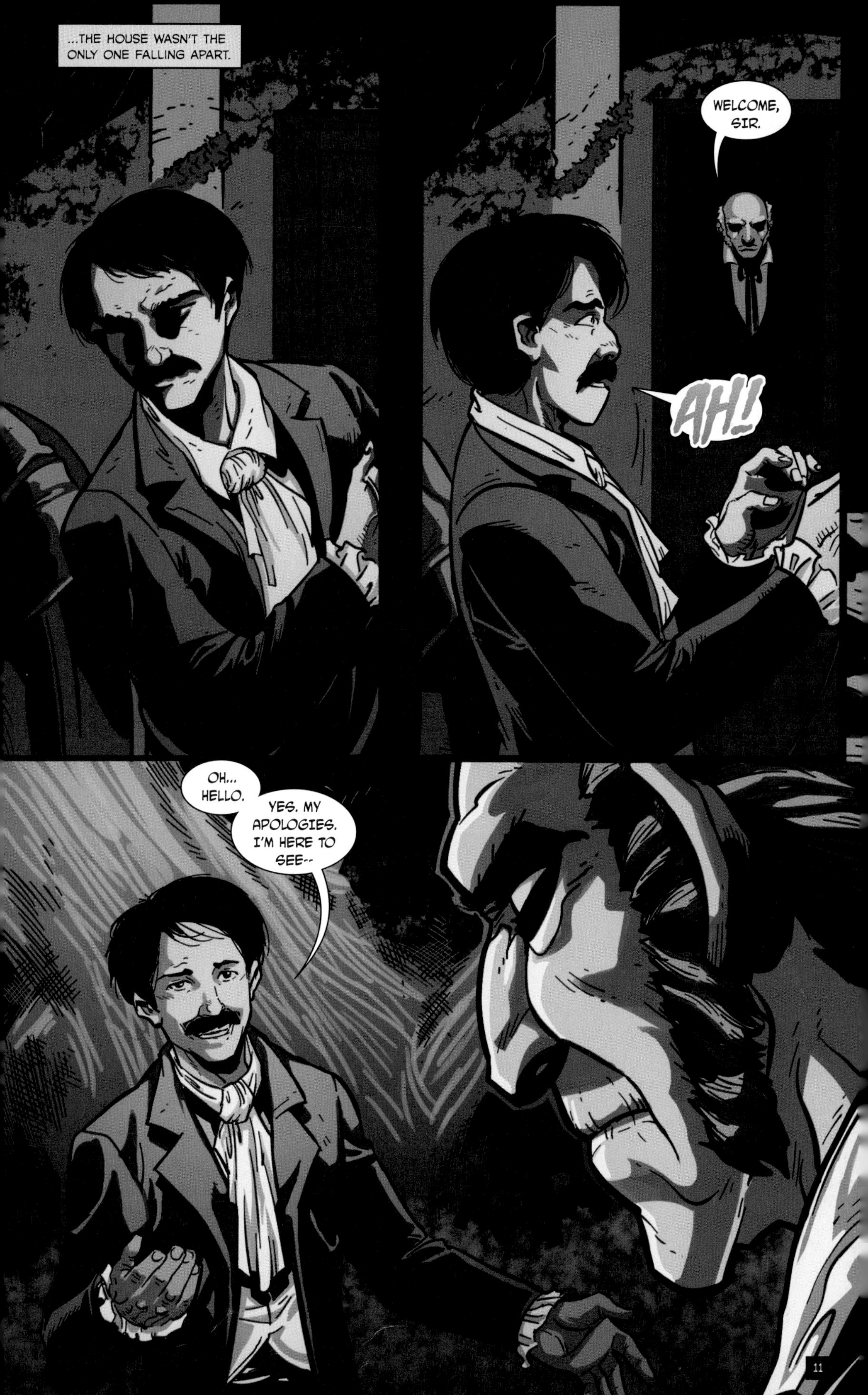
...THE HOUSE WASN'T THE ONLY ONE FALLING APART.
WELCOME, SIR.
AH!
OH... HELLO.
YES. MY APOLOGIES. I'M HERE TO SEE--

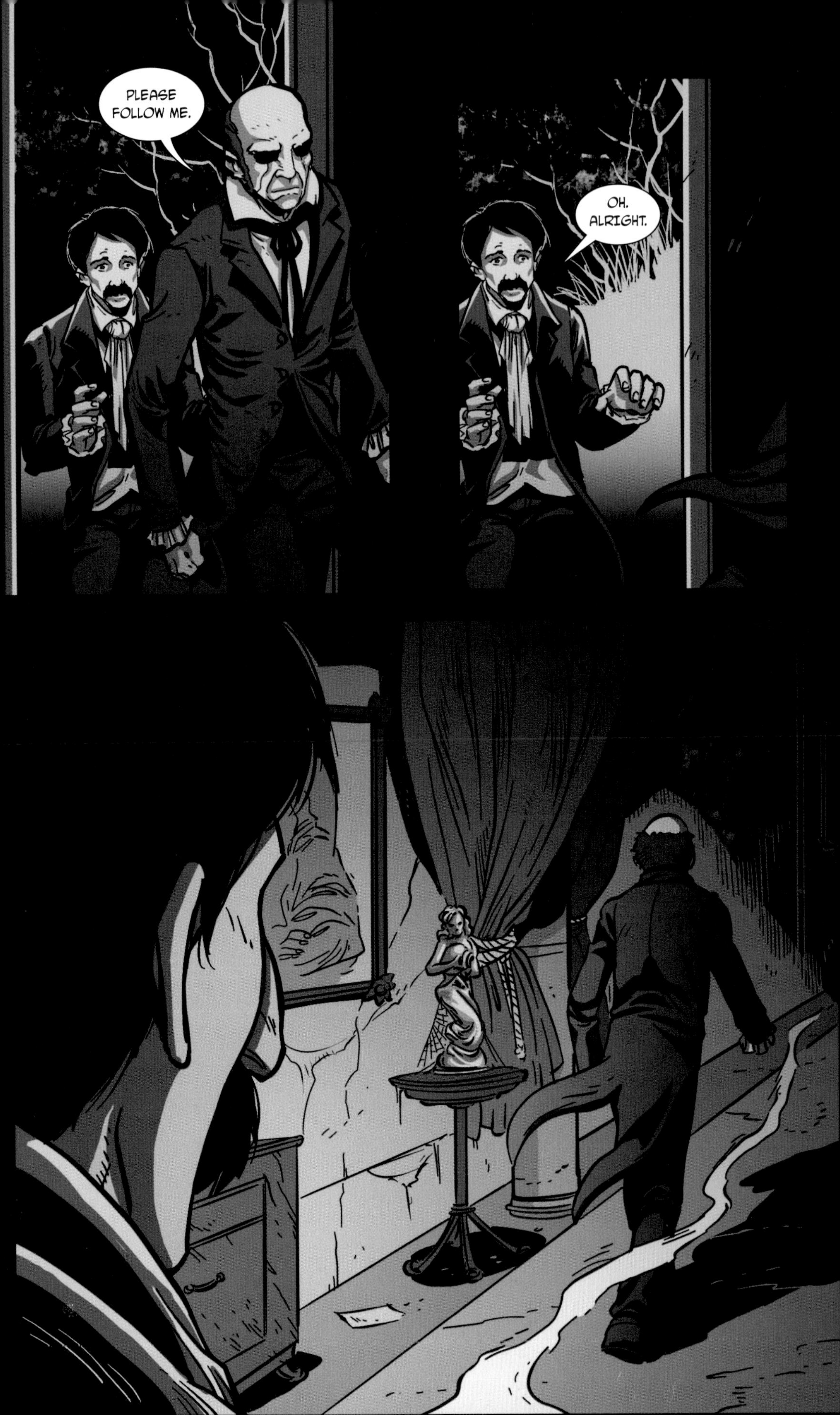
PLEASE FOLLOW ME.
OH. ALRIGHT.

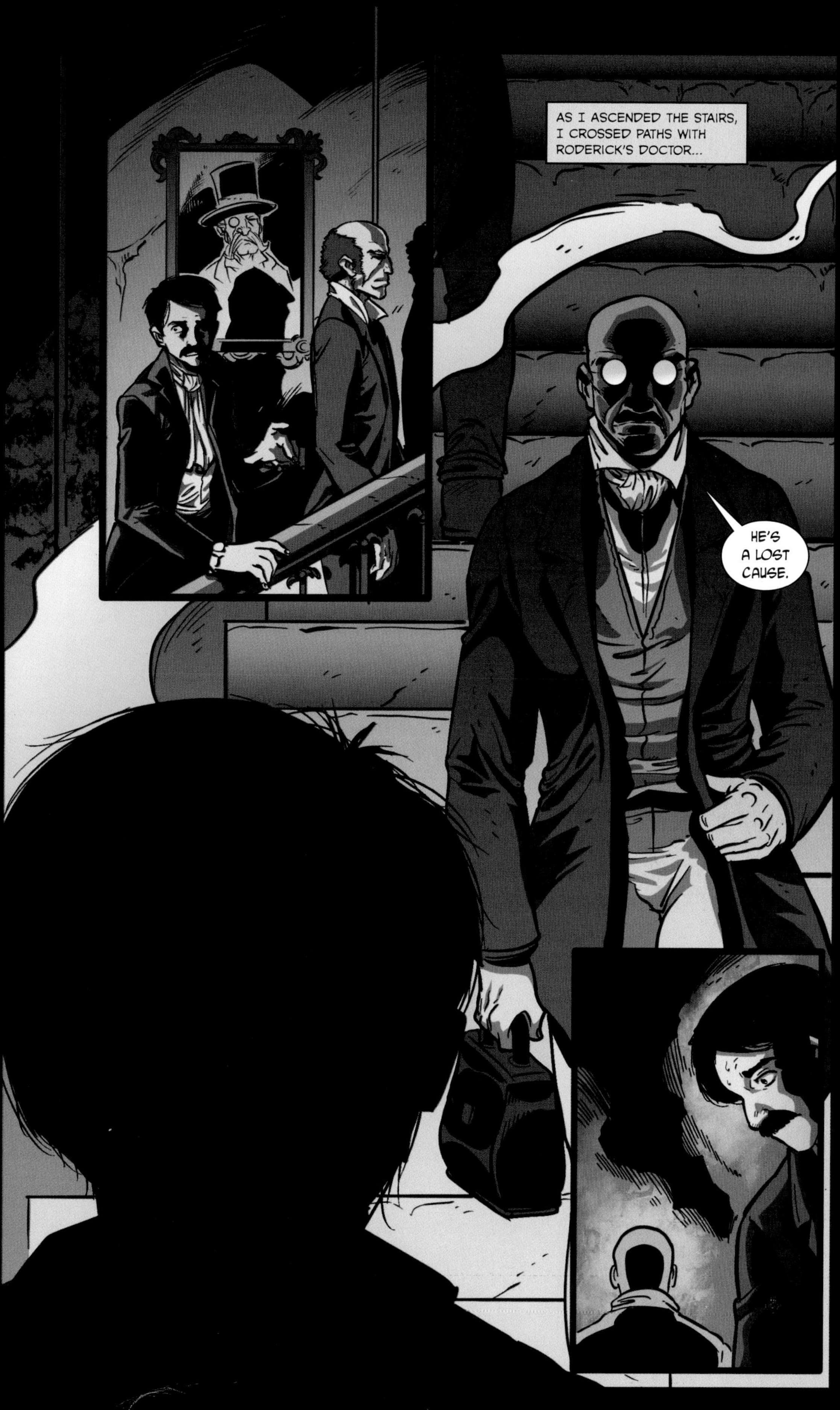
AS I ASCENDED THE STAIRS, I CROSSED PATHS WITH RODERICK'S DOCTOR...
HE'S A LOST CAUSE.

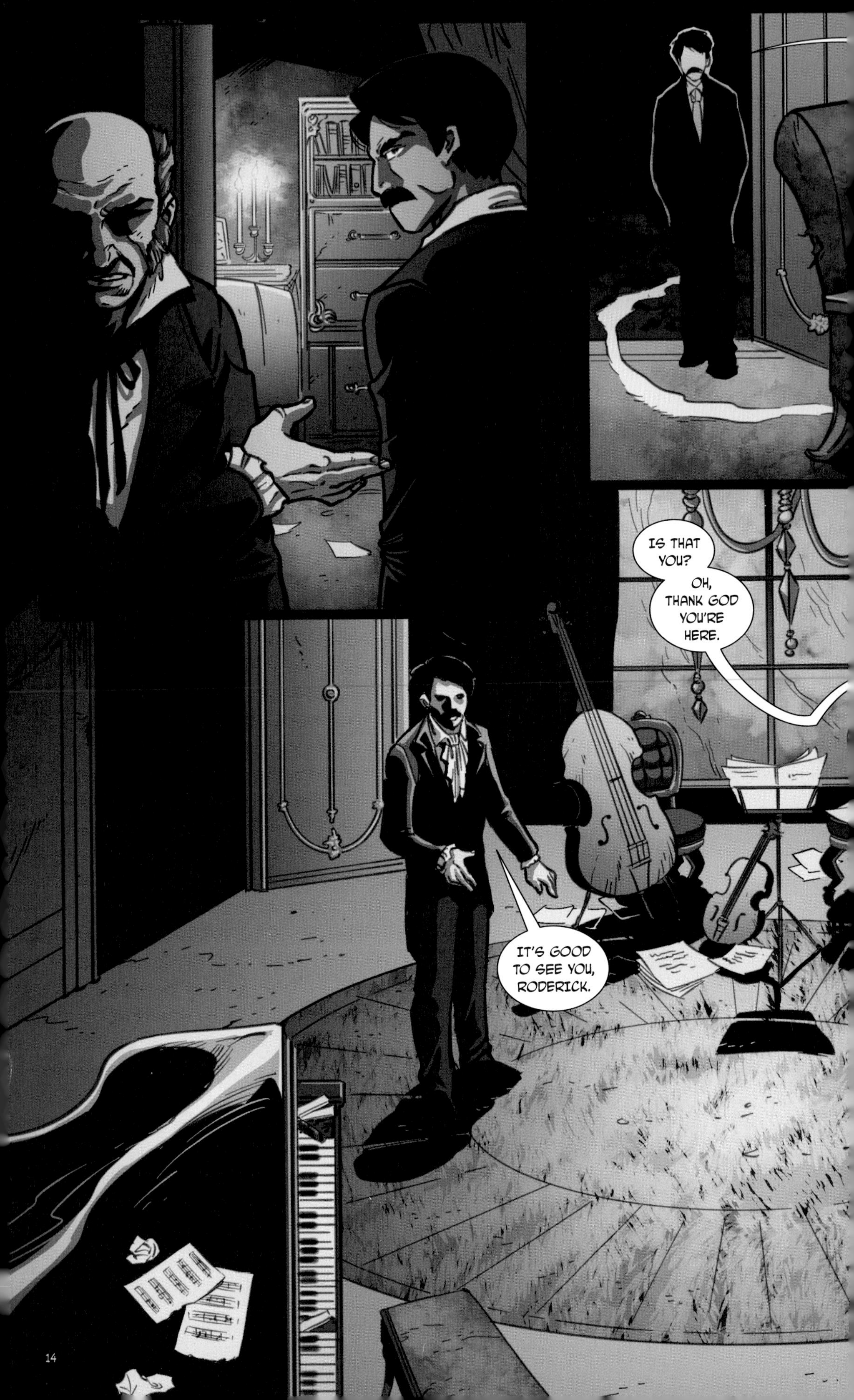

IS THAT YOU?
OH, THANK GOD YOU'RE HERE.
IT'S GOOD TO SEE YOU, RODERICK.

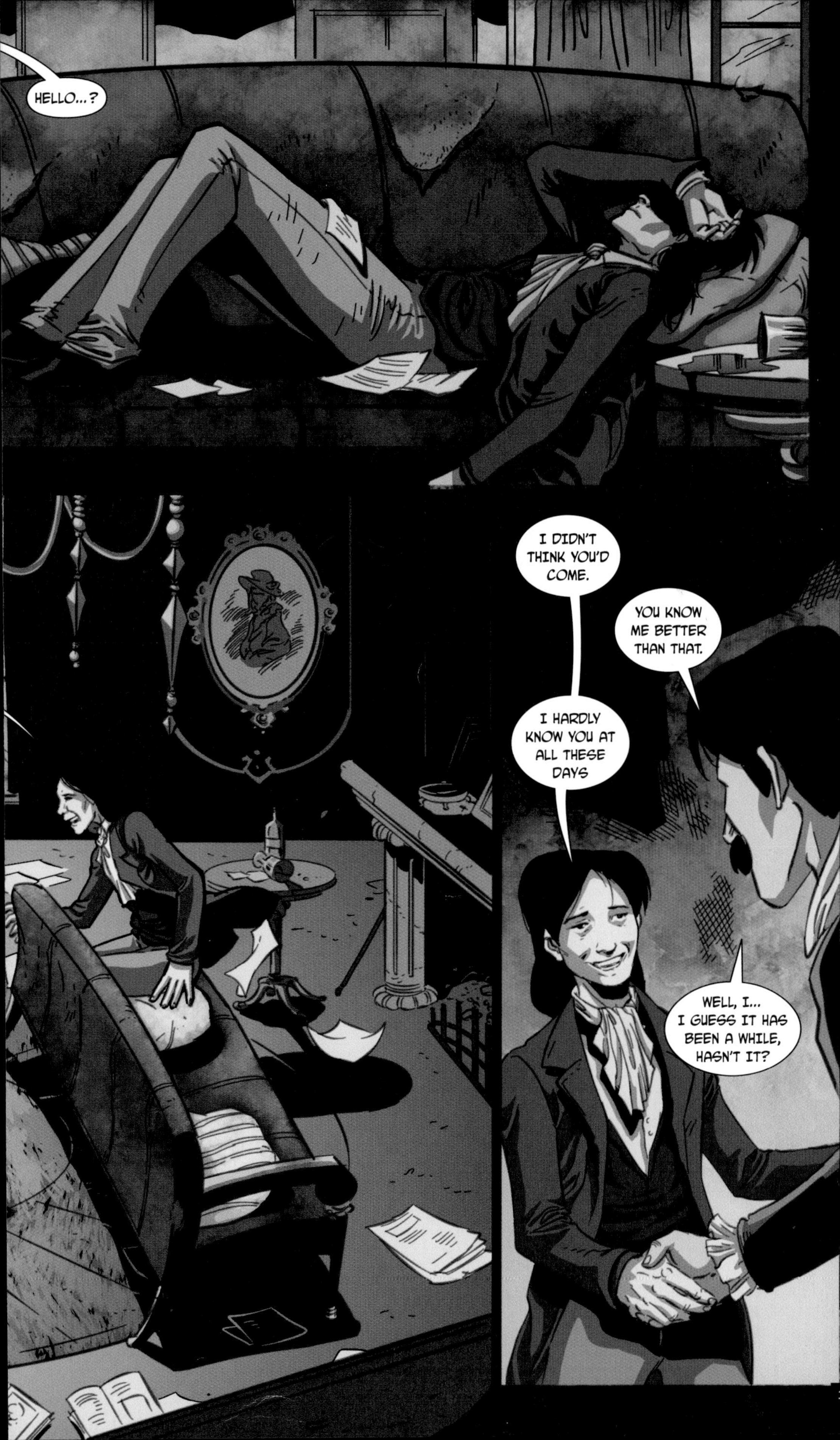
HELLO...?
I DIDN'T THINK YOU'D COME.
YOU KNOW ME BETTER THAN THAT.
I HARDLY KNOW YOU AT ALL THESE DAYS
WELL, I... I GUESS IT HAS BEEN A WHILE, HASN'T IT?

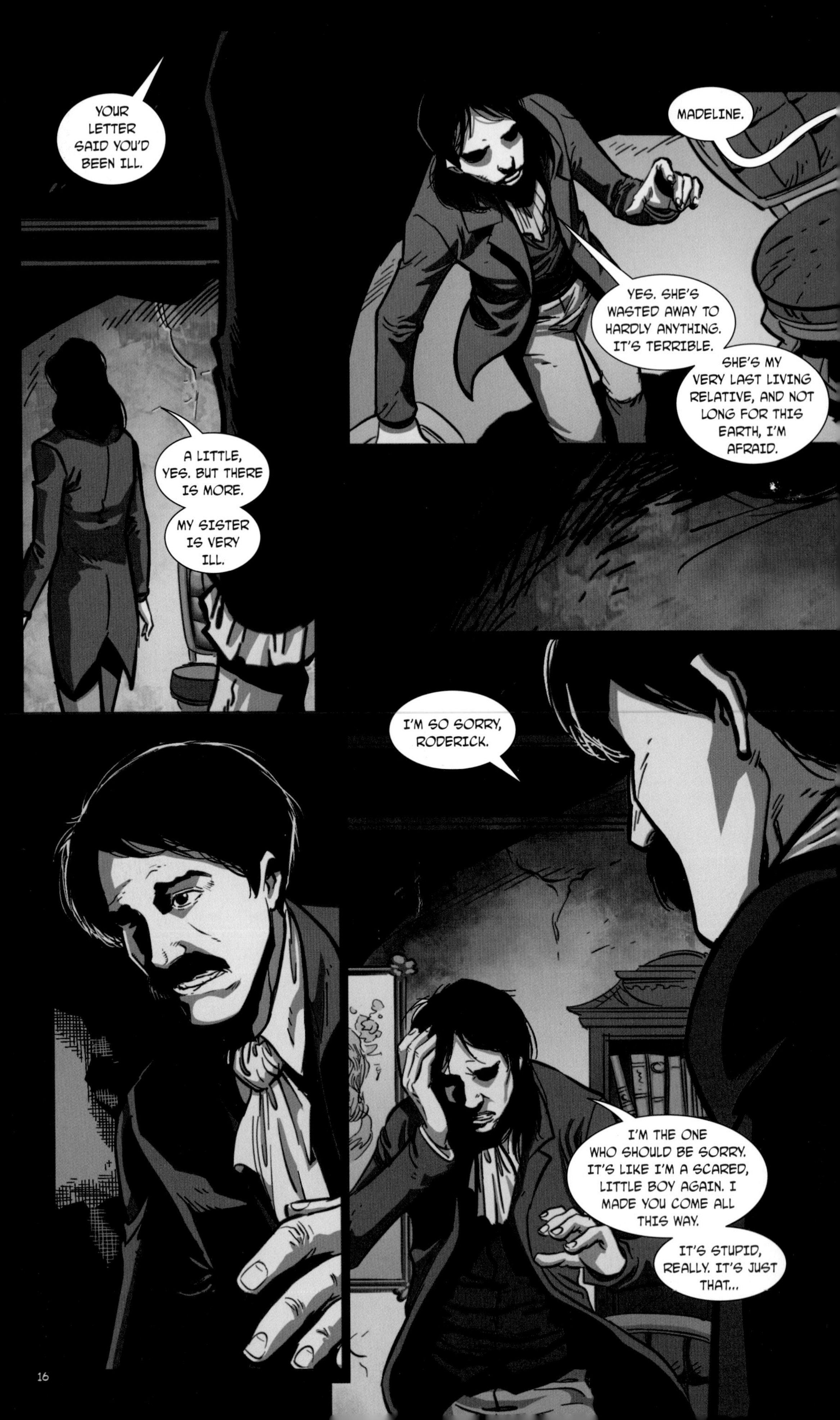
YOUR LETTER SAID YOU'D BEEN ILL.
A LITTLE, YES. BUT THERE IS MORE.
MY SISTER IS VERY ILL.
MADELINE.
YES. SHE'S WASTED AWAY TO HARDLY ANYTHING. IT'S TERRIBLE.
SHE'S MY VERY LAST LIVING RELATIVE, AND NOT LONG FOR THIS EARTH, I'M AFRAID.
I'M SO SORRY, RODERICK.
I'M THE ONE WHO SHOULD BE SORRY. IT'S LIKE I'M A SCARED, LITTLE BOY AGAIN. I MADE YOU COME ALL THIS WAY.
IT'S STUPID, REALLY. IT'S JUST THAT...

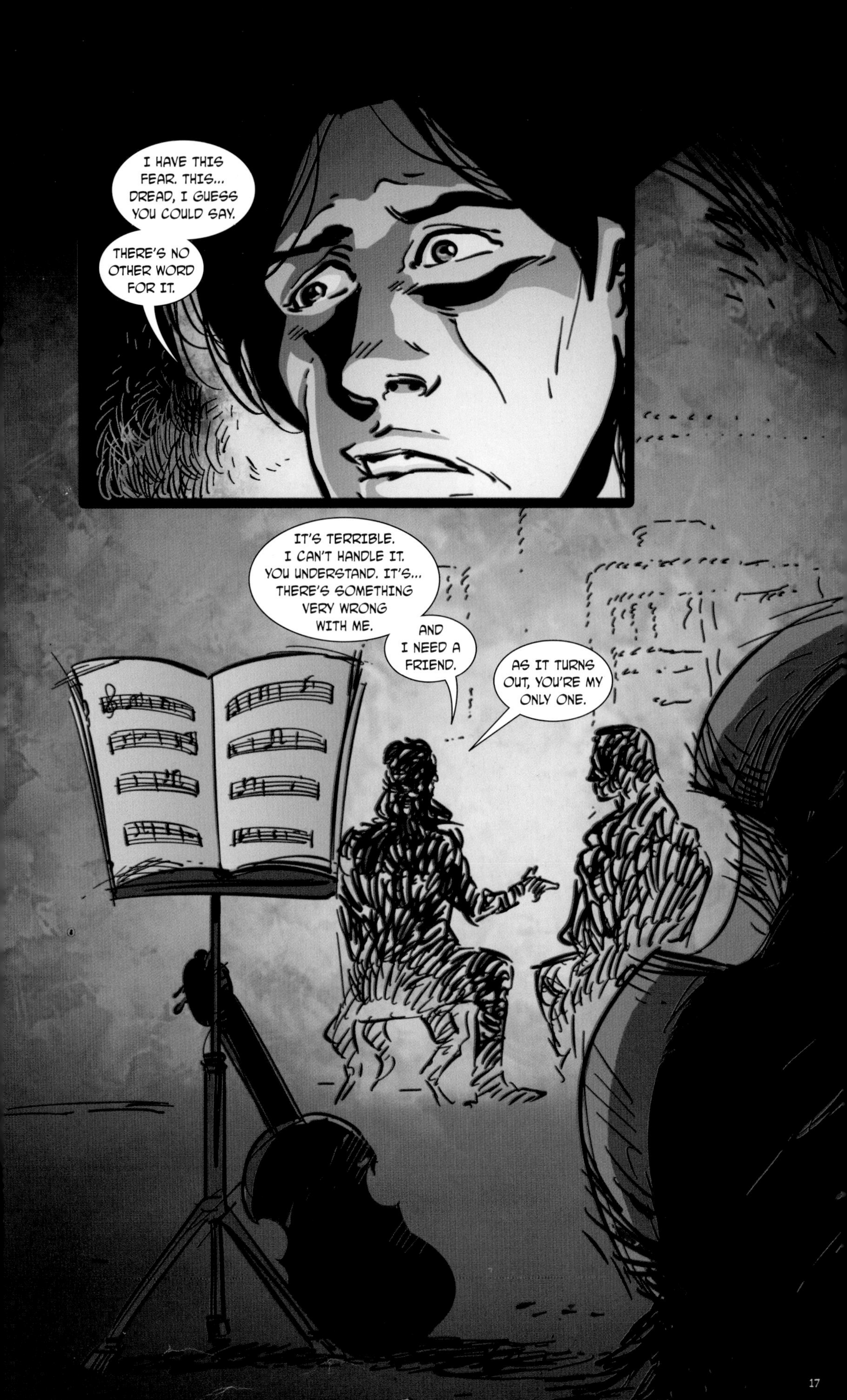
I HAVE THIS FEAR. THIS... DREAD, I GUESS YOU COULD SAY.
THERE'S NO OTHER WORD FOR IT.
IT'S TERRIBLE. I CAN'T HANDLE IT. YOU UNDERSTAND. IT'S... THERE'S SOMETHING VERY WRONG WITH ME.
AND I NEED A FRIEND.
AS IT TURNS OUT, YOU'RE MY ONLY ONE.

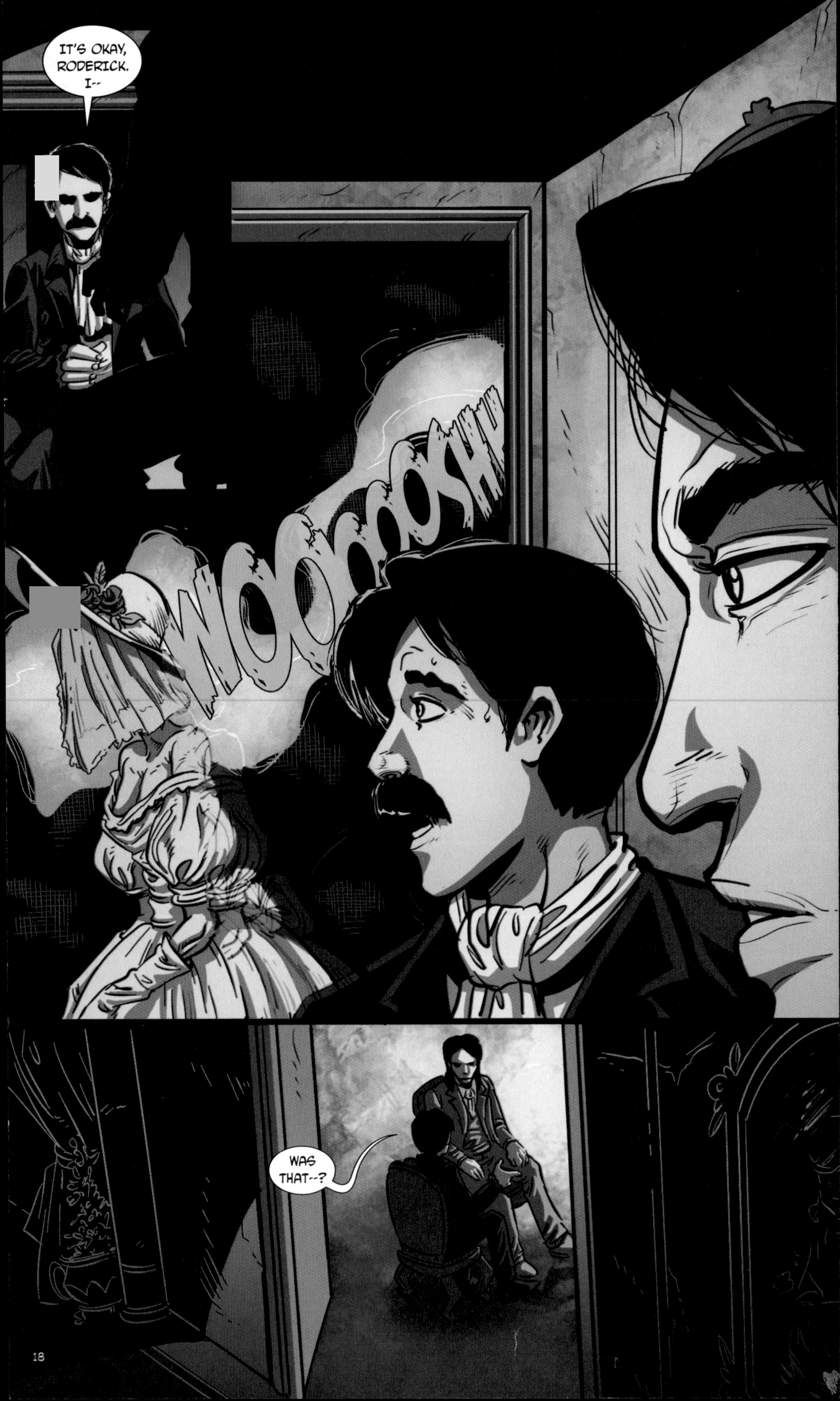
IT'S OKAY, RODERICK. I--
WOOOOOSH!
WAS THAT--?

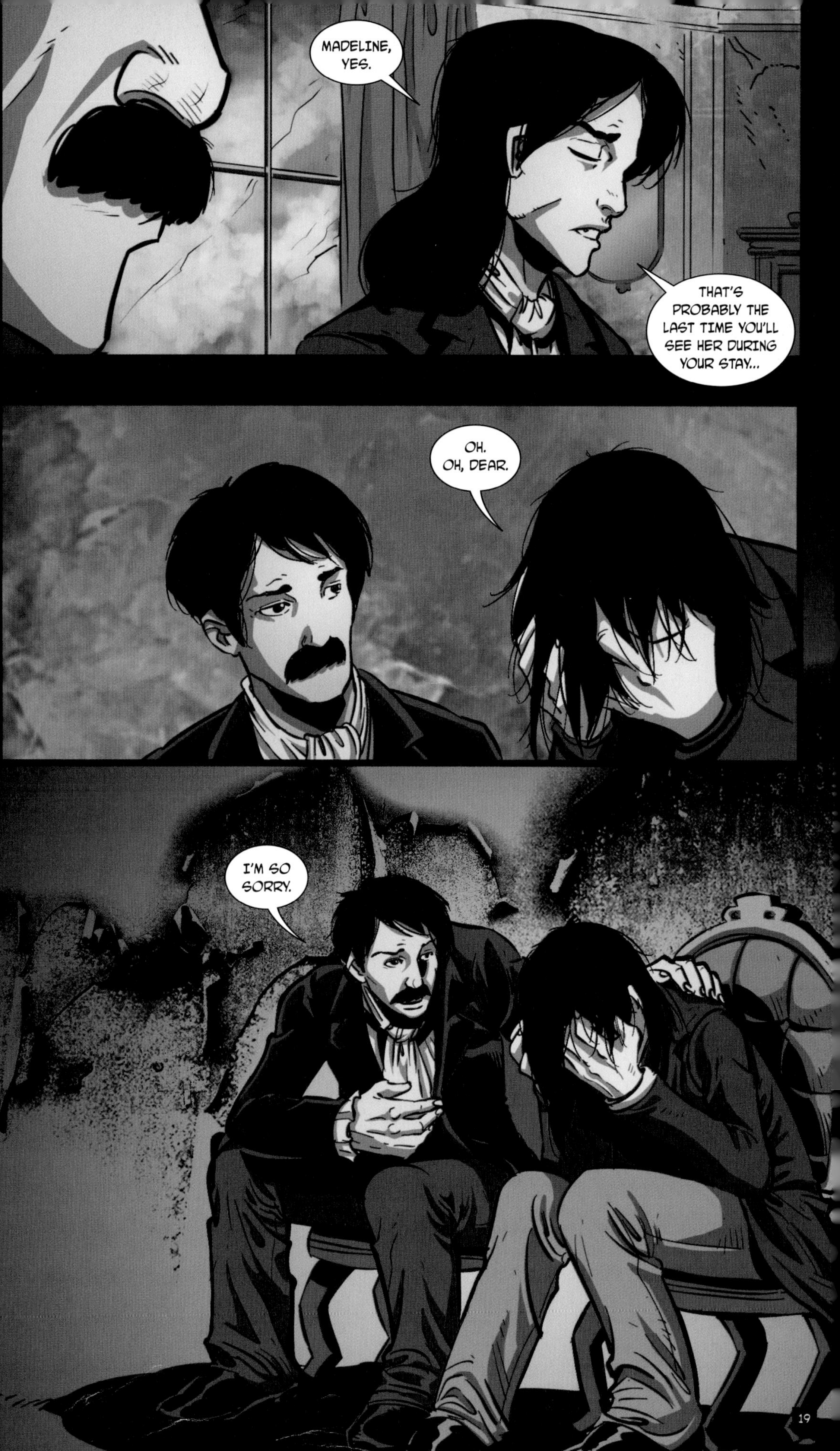
MADELINE, YES.
THAT'S PROBABLY THE LAST TIME YOU'LL SEE HER DURING YOUR STAY...
OH. OH, DEAR.
I'M SO SORRY.

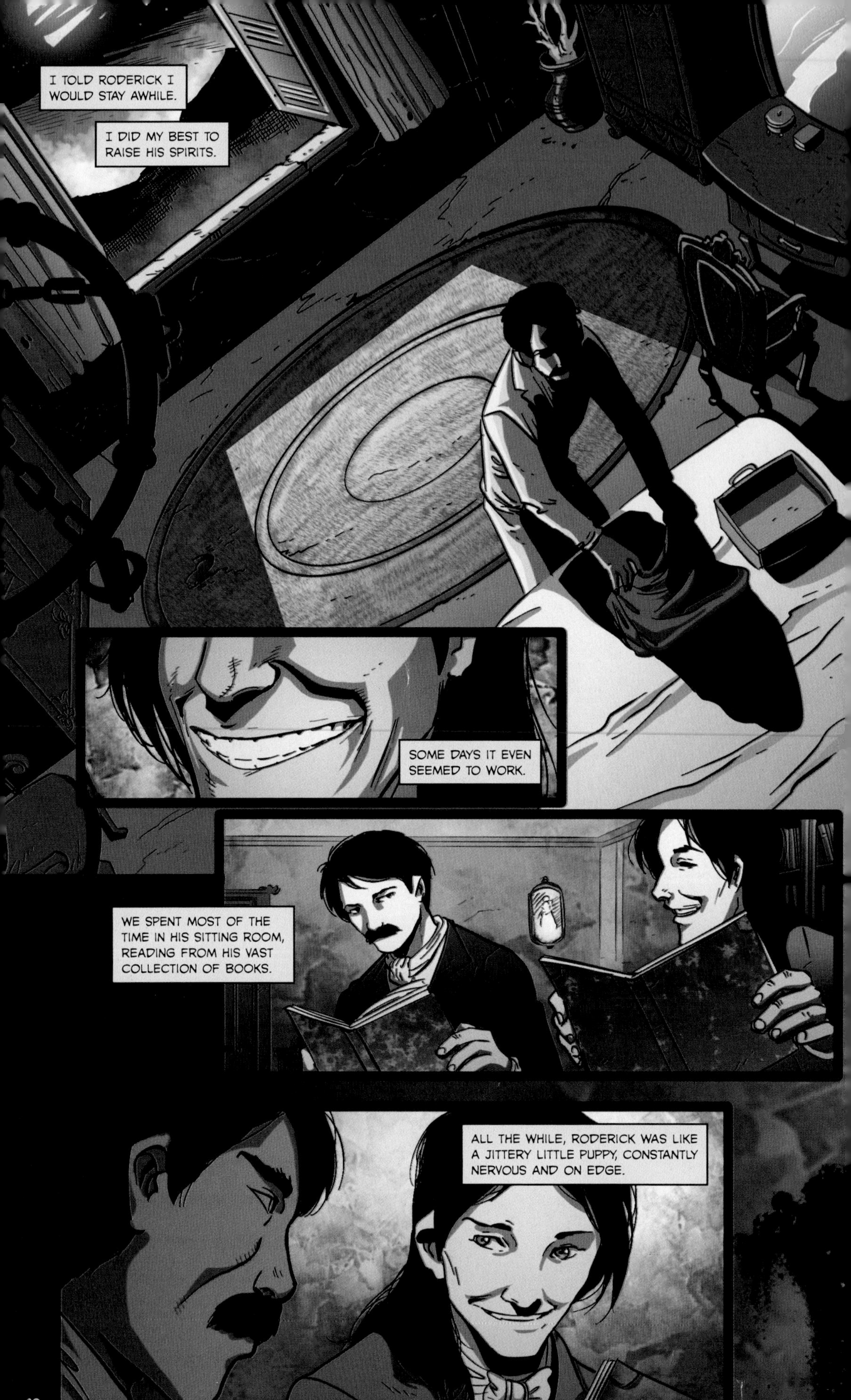
I TOLD RODERICK I WOULD STAY AWHILE.
I DID MY BEST TO RAISE HIS SPIRITS.
SOME DAYS IT EVEN SEEMED TO WORK.
WE SPENT MOST OF THE TIME IN HIS SITTING ROOM, READING FROM HIS VAST COLLECTION OF BOOKS.
ALL THE WHILE, RODERICK WAS LIKE A JITTERY LITTLE PUPPY, CONSTANTLY NERVOUS AND ON EDGE.

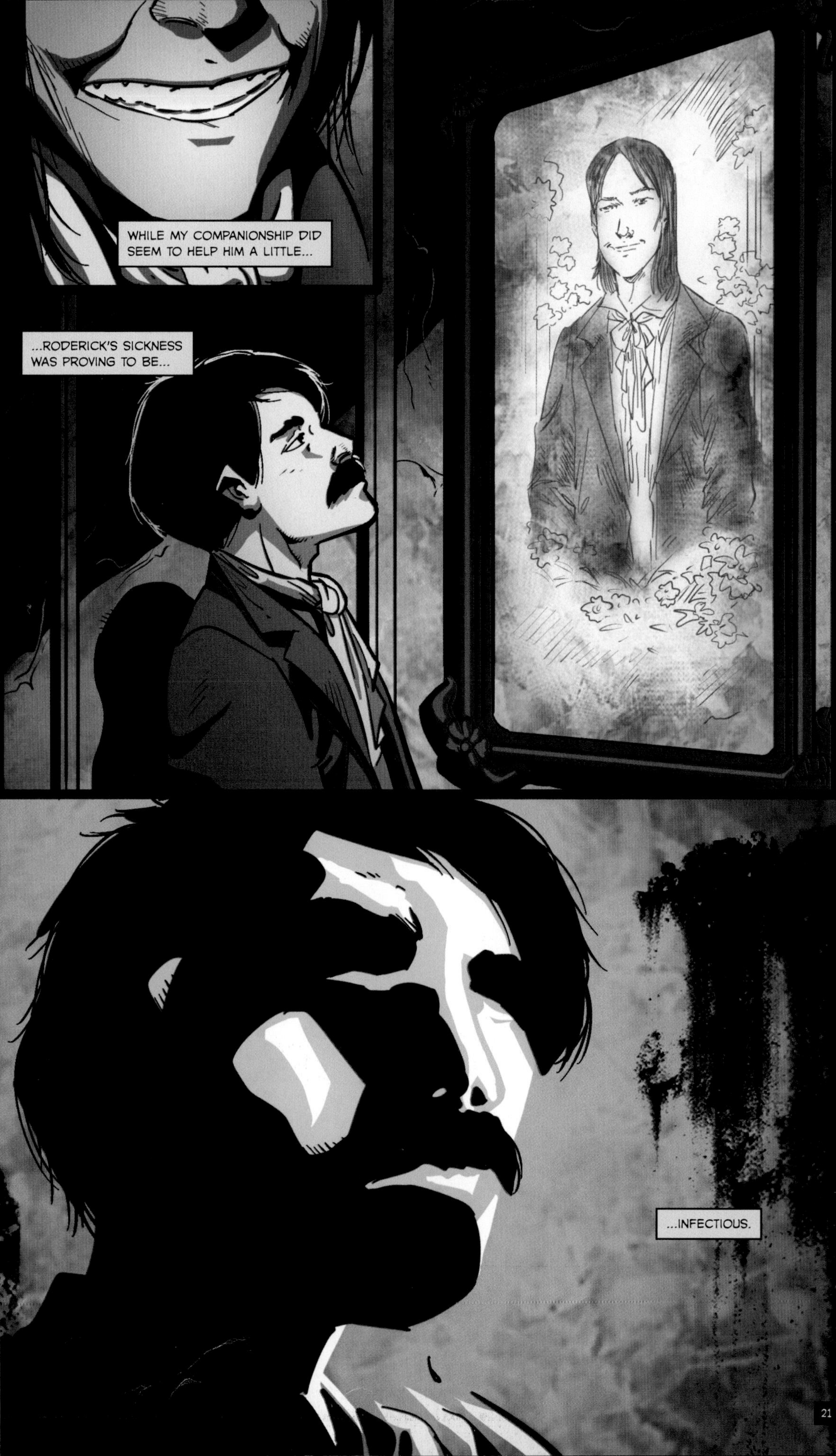
WHILE MY COMPANIONSHIP DID SEEM TO HELP HIM A LITTLE...
...RODERICK'S SICKNESS WAS PROVING TO BE...
...INFECTIOUS.

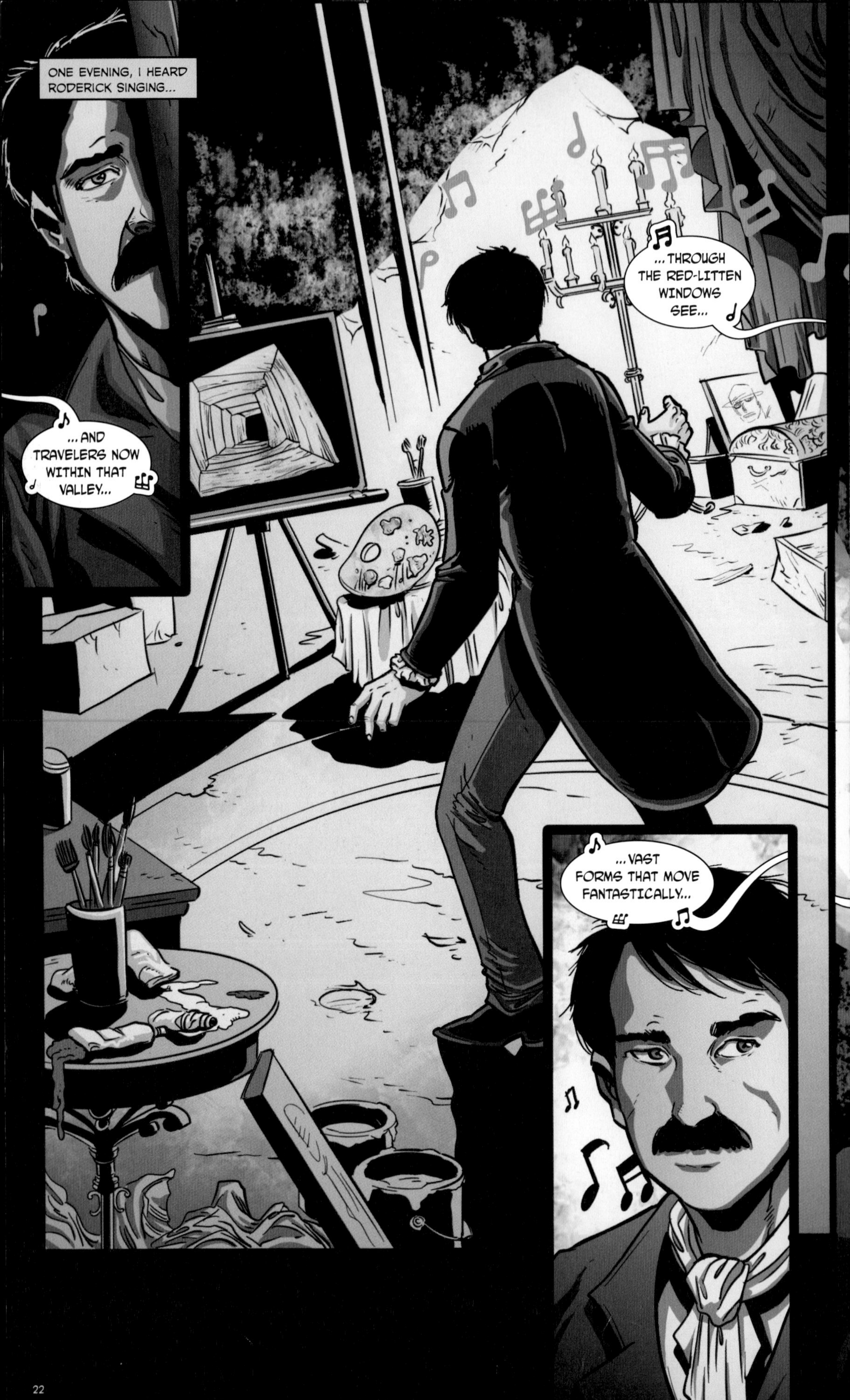
ONE EVENING, I HEARD RODERICK SINGING...
...AND TRAVELERS NOW WITHIN THAT VALLEY...
...THROUGH THE RED-LITTEN WINDOWS SEE...
...VAST FORMS THAT MOVE FANTASTICALLY...

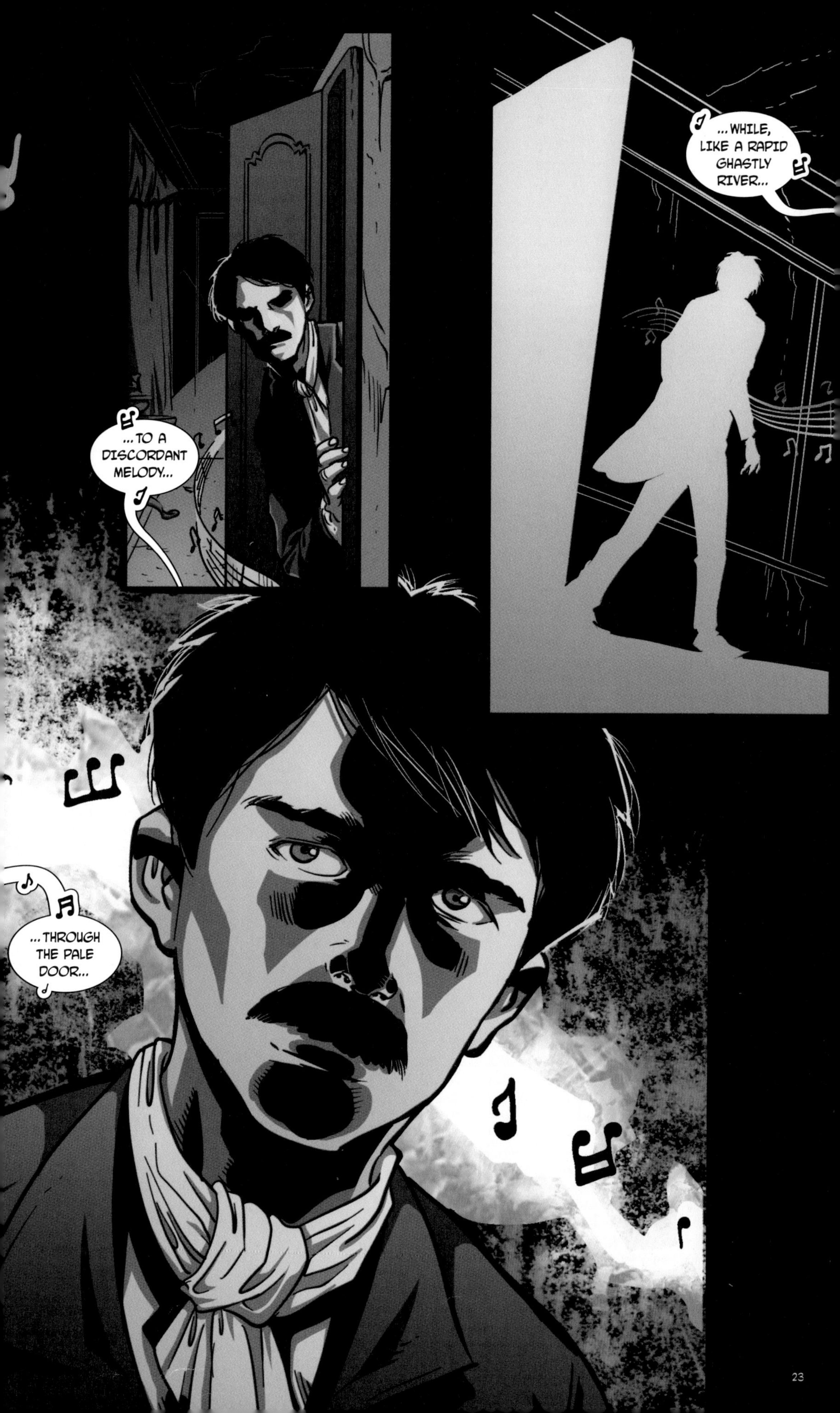
...TO A DISCORDANT MELODY...
...WHILE, LIKE A RAPID GHASTLY RIVER...
...THROUGH THE PALE DOOR...

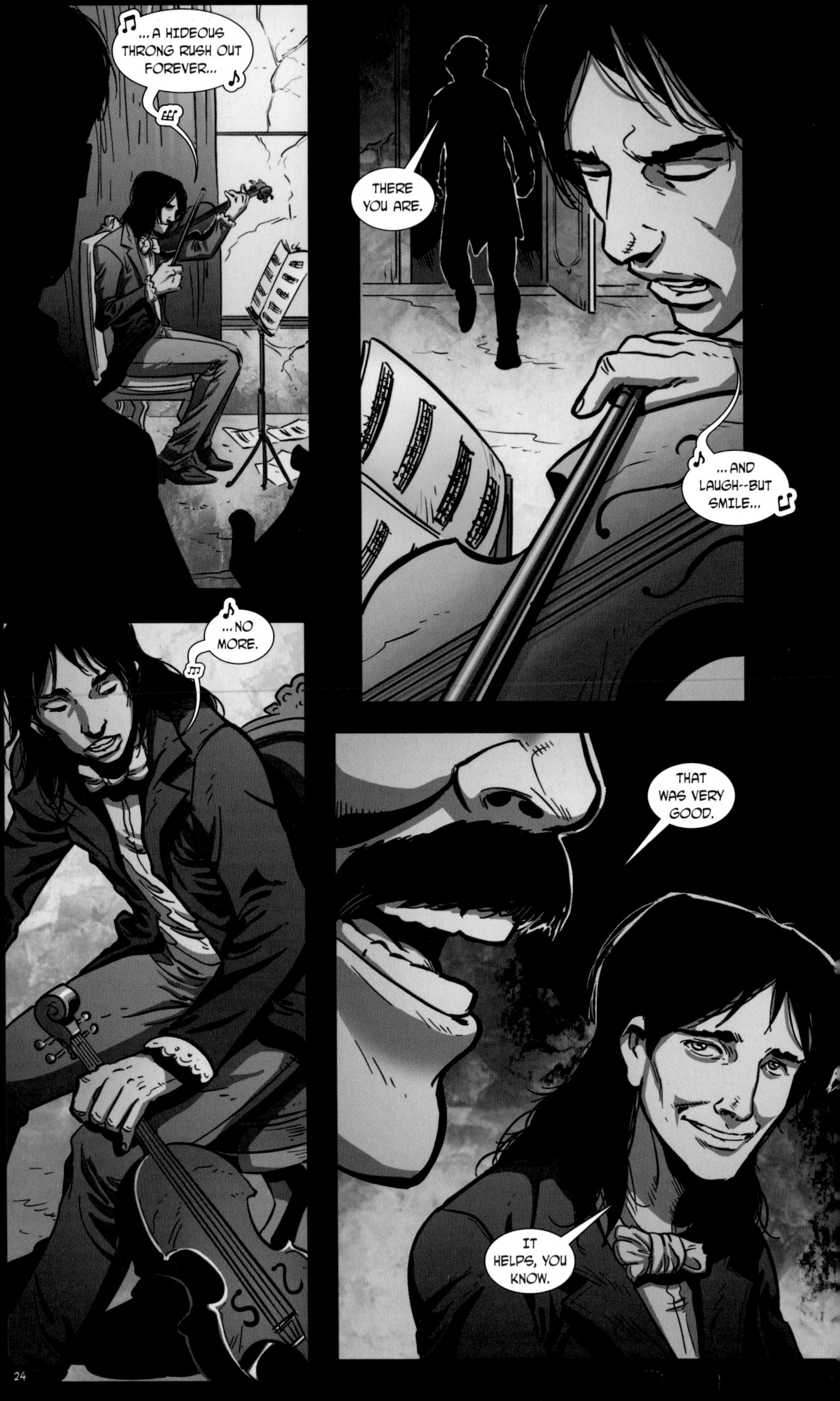
...A HIDEOUS THRONG RUSH OUT FOREVER...
THERE YOU ARE.
...AND LAUGH--BUT SMILE...
...NO MORE.
THAT WAS VERY GOOD.
IT HELPS, YOU KNOW.

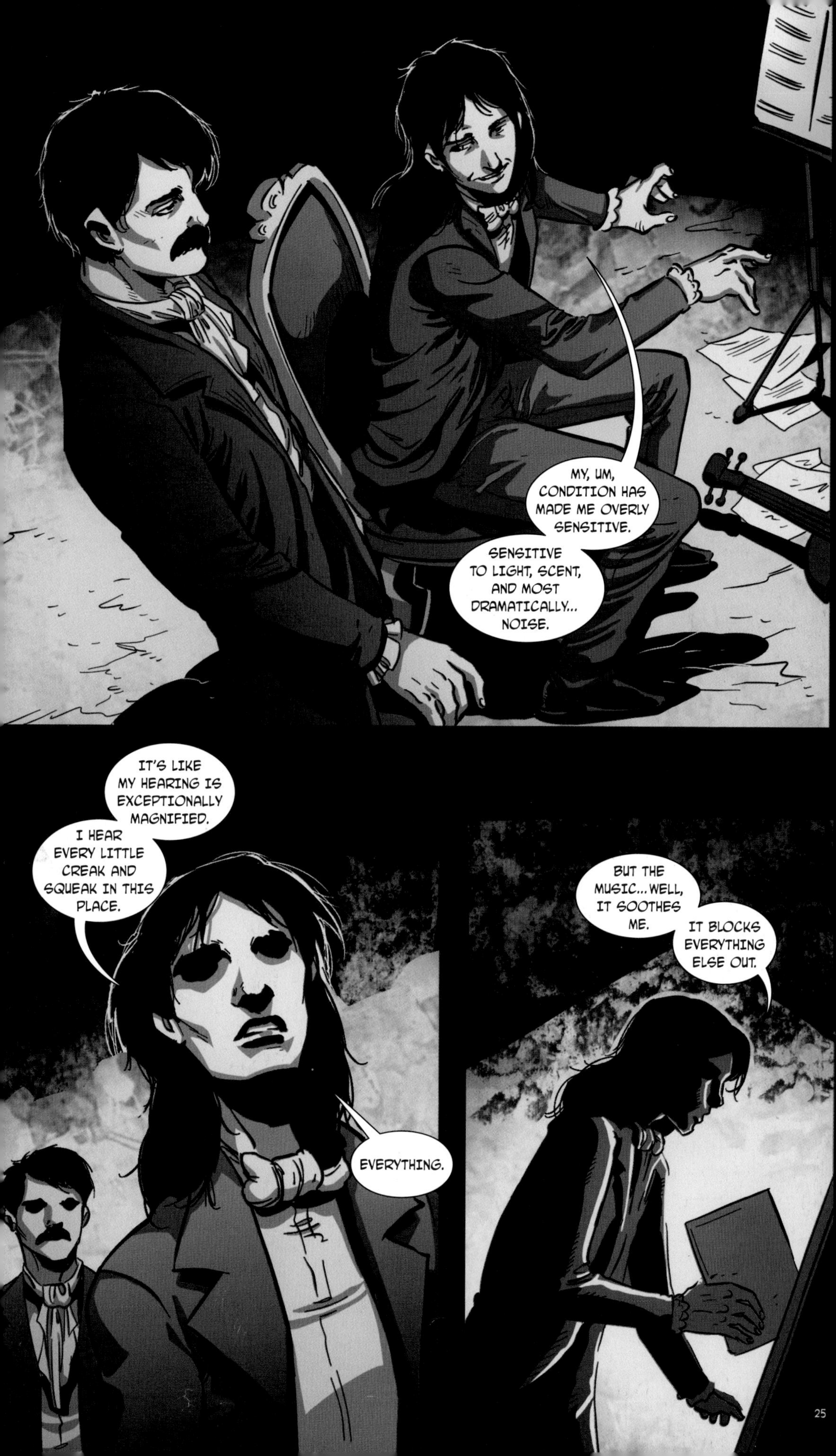

MY, UM, CONDITION HAS MADE ME OVERLY SENSITIVE.
SENSITIVE TO LIGHT, SCENT, AND MOST DRAMATICALLY... NOISE.
IT'S LIKE MY HEARING IS EXCEPTIONALLY MAGNIFIED.
I HEAR EVERY LITTLE CREAK AND SQUEAK IN THIS PLACE.
EVERYTHING.
BUT THE MUSIC... WELL, IT SOOTHES ME.
IT BLOCKS EVERYTHING ELSE OUT.

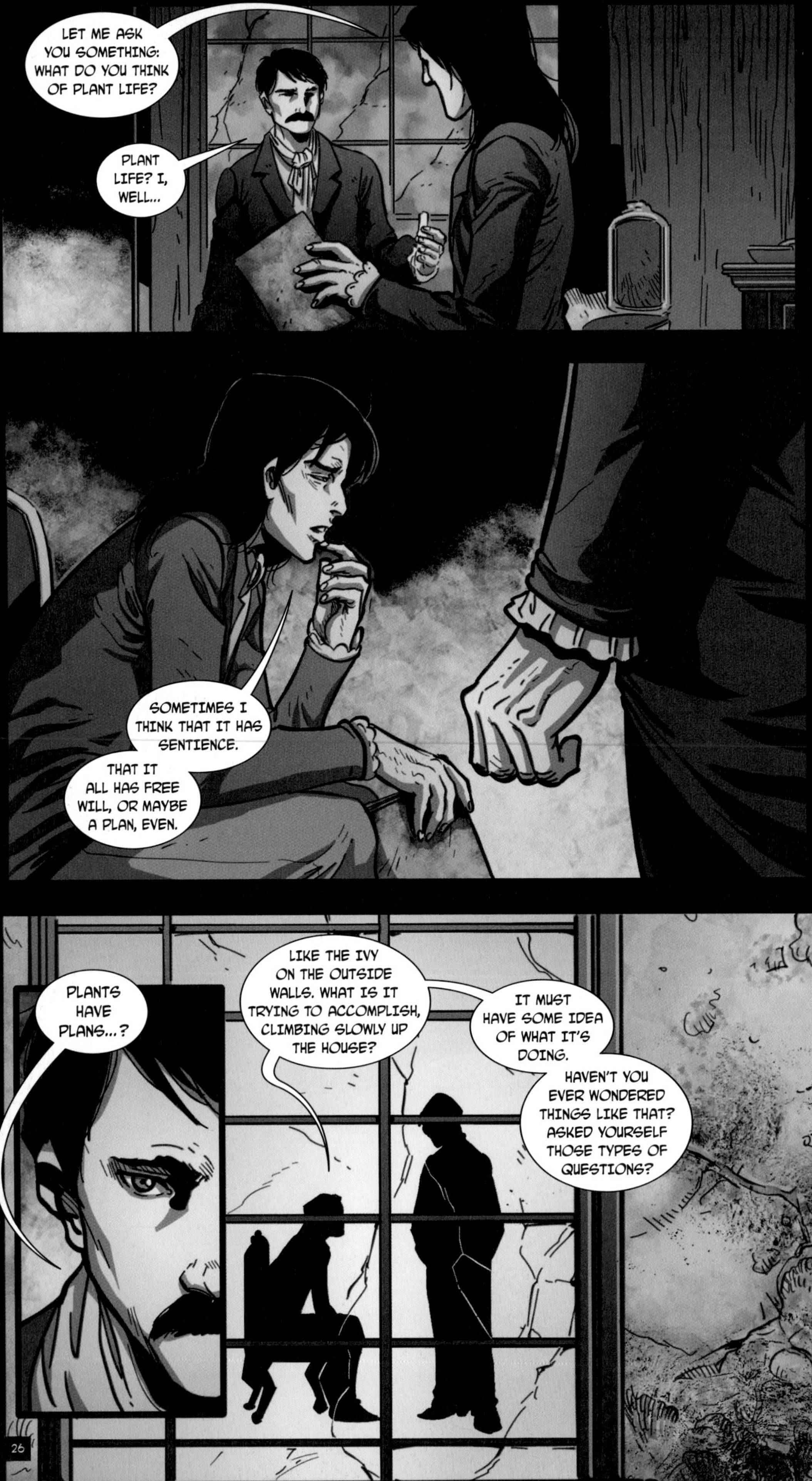
LET ME ASK YOU SOMETHING: WHAT DO YOU THINK OF PLANT LIFE?
PLANT LIFE? I, WELL...
SOMETIMES I THINK THAT IT HAS SENTIENCE.
THAT IT ALL HAS FREE WILL, OR MAYBE A PLAN, EVEN.
PLANTS HAVE PLANS...?
LIKE THE IVY ON THE OUTSIDE WALLS. WHAT IS IT TRYING TO ACCOMPLISH, CLIMBING SLOWLY UP THE HOUSE?
IT MUST HAVE SOME IDEA OF WHAT IT'S DOING.
HAVEN'T YOU EVER WONDERED THINGS LIKE THAT? ASKED YOURSELF THOSE TYPES OF QUESTIONS?

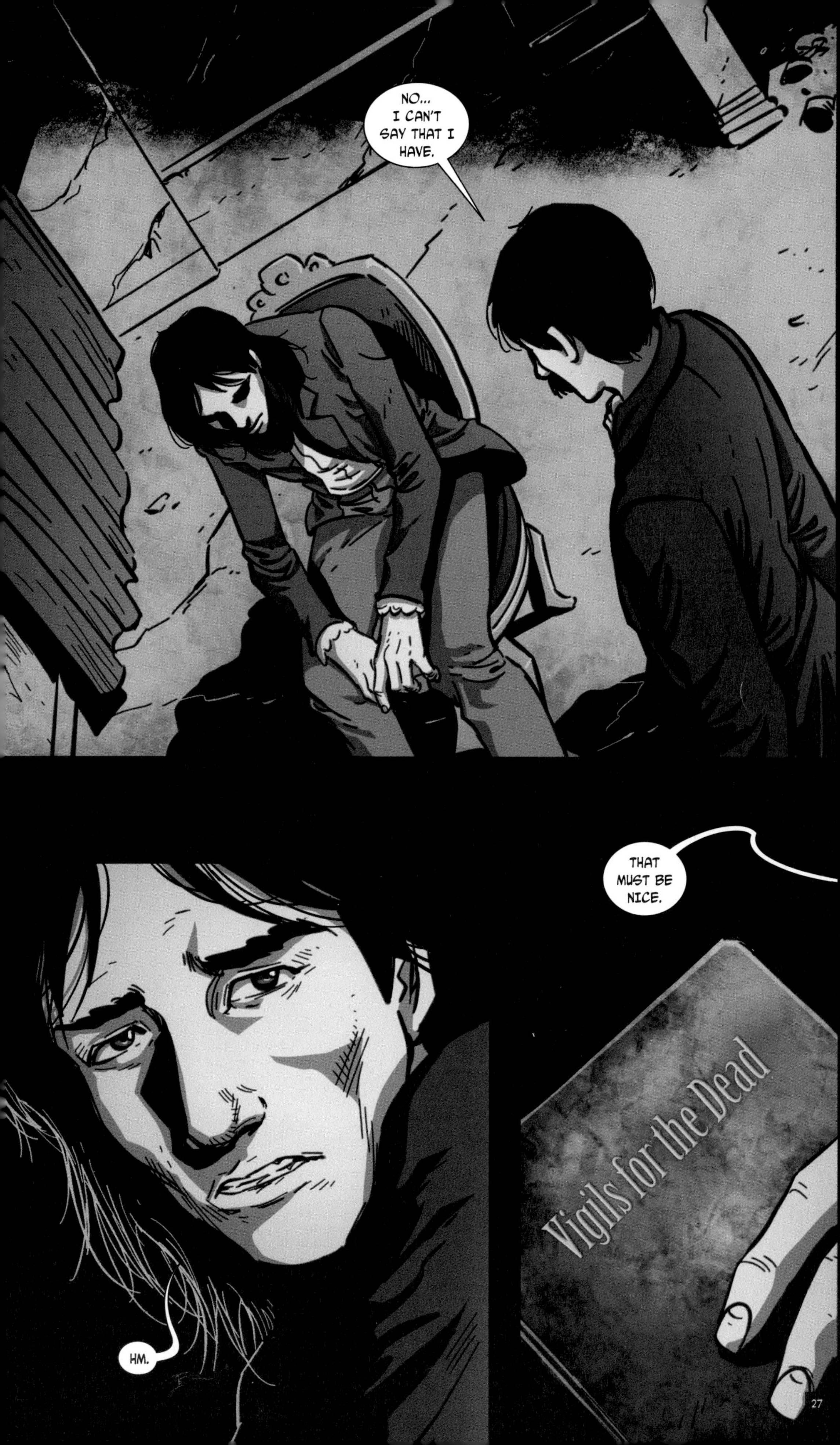
NO... I CAN'T SAY THAT I HAVE.
THAT MUST BE NICE.
HM.
Vigils for the Dead

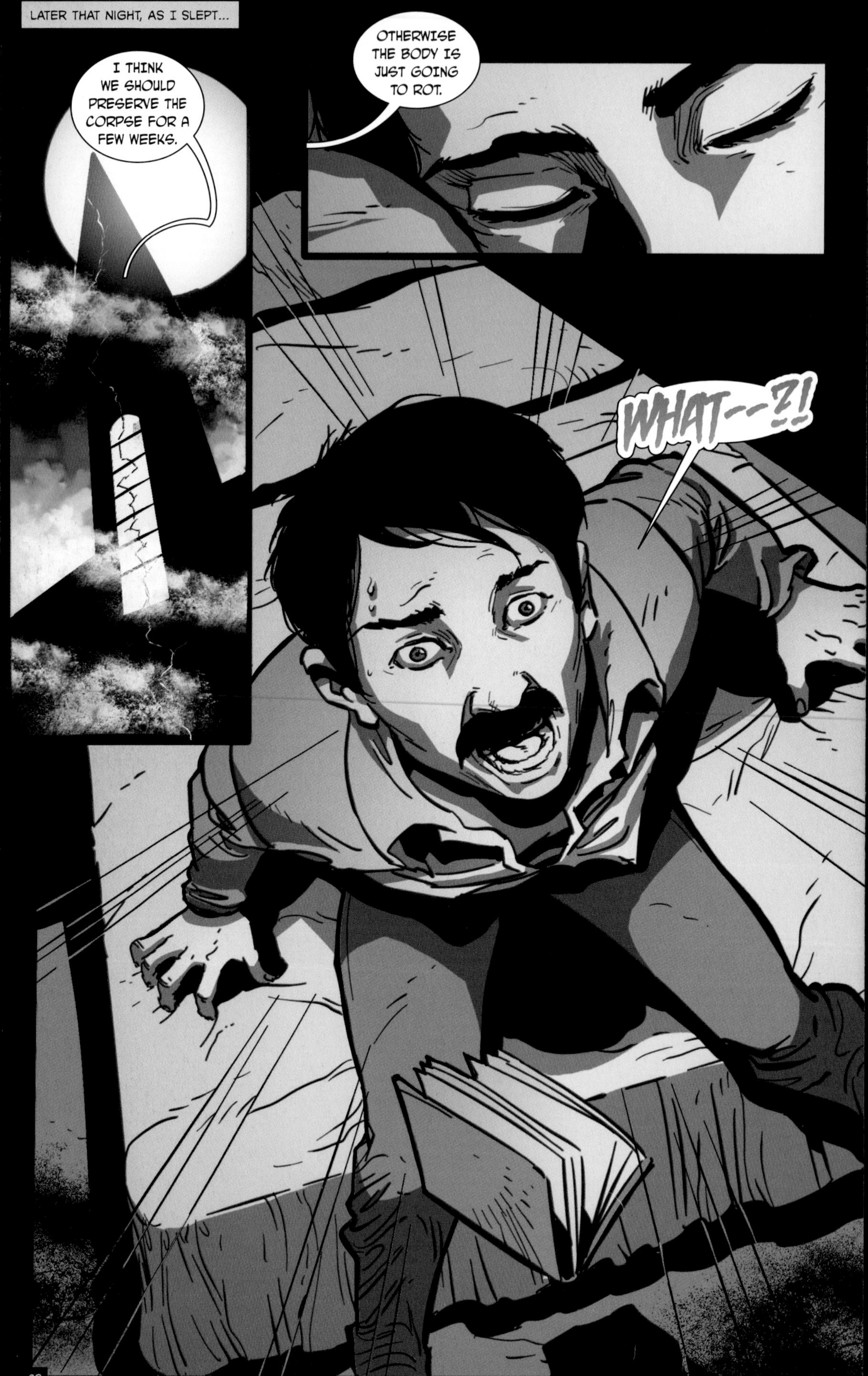
LATER THAT NIGHT, AS I SLEPT...
I THINK WE SHOULD PRESERVE THE CORPSE FOR A FEW WEEKS.
OTHERWISE THE BODY IS JUST GOING TO ROT.
WHAT--?!

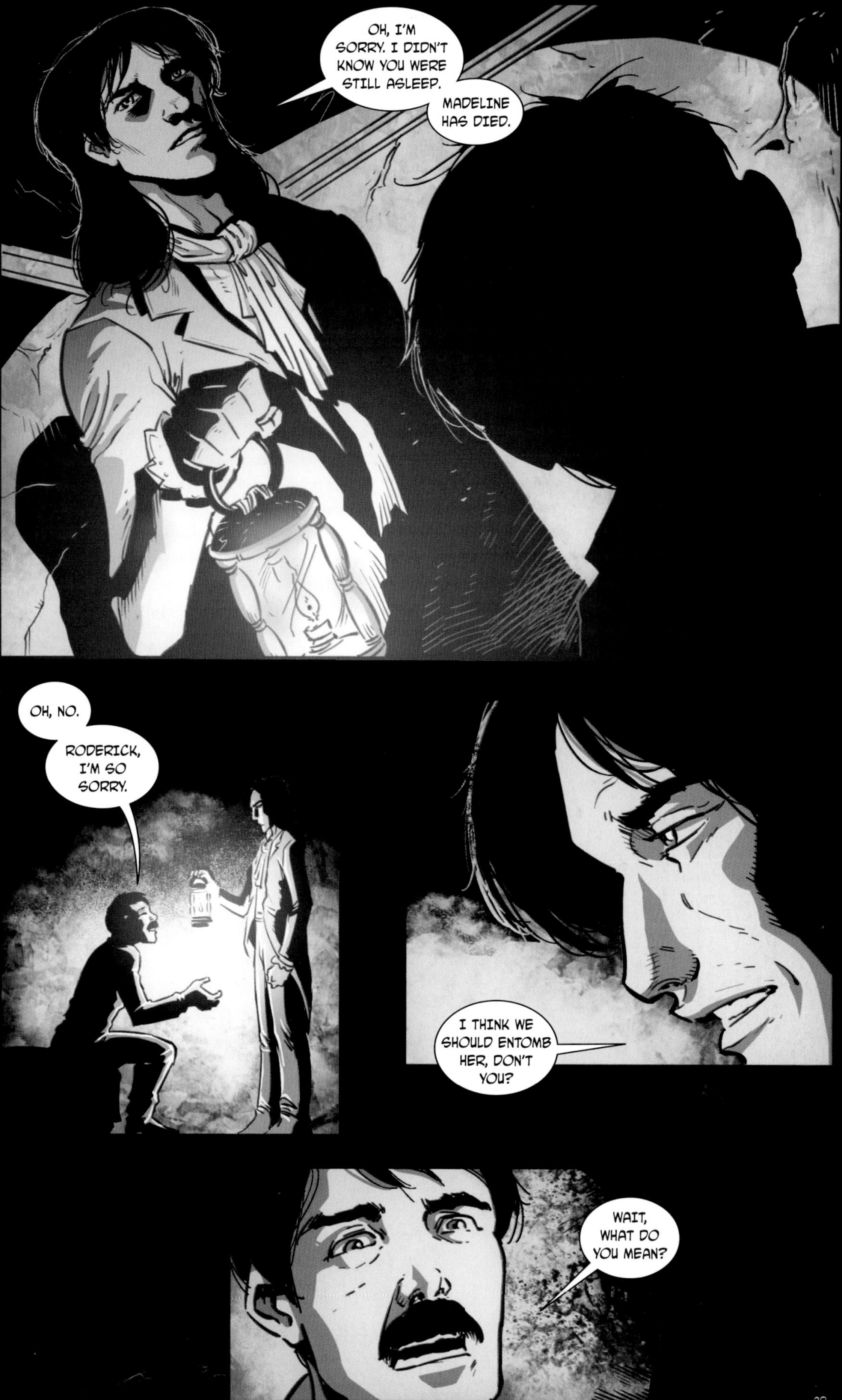
OH, I'M SORRY. I DIDN'T KNOW YOU WERE STILL ASLEEP.
MADELINE HAS DIED.
OH, NO.
RODERICK, I'M SO SORRY.
I THINK WE SHOULD ENTOMB HER, DON'T YOU?
WAIT, WHAT DO YOU MEAN?

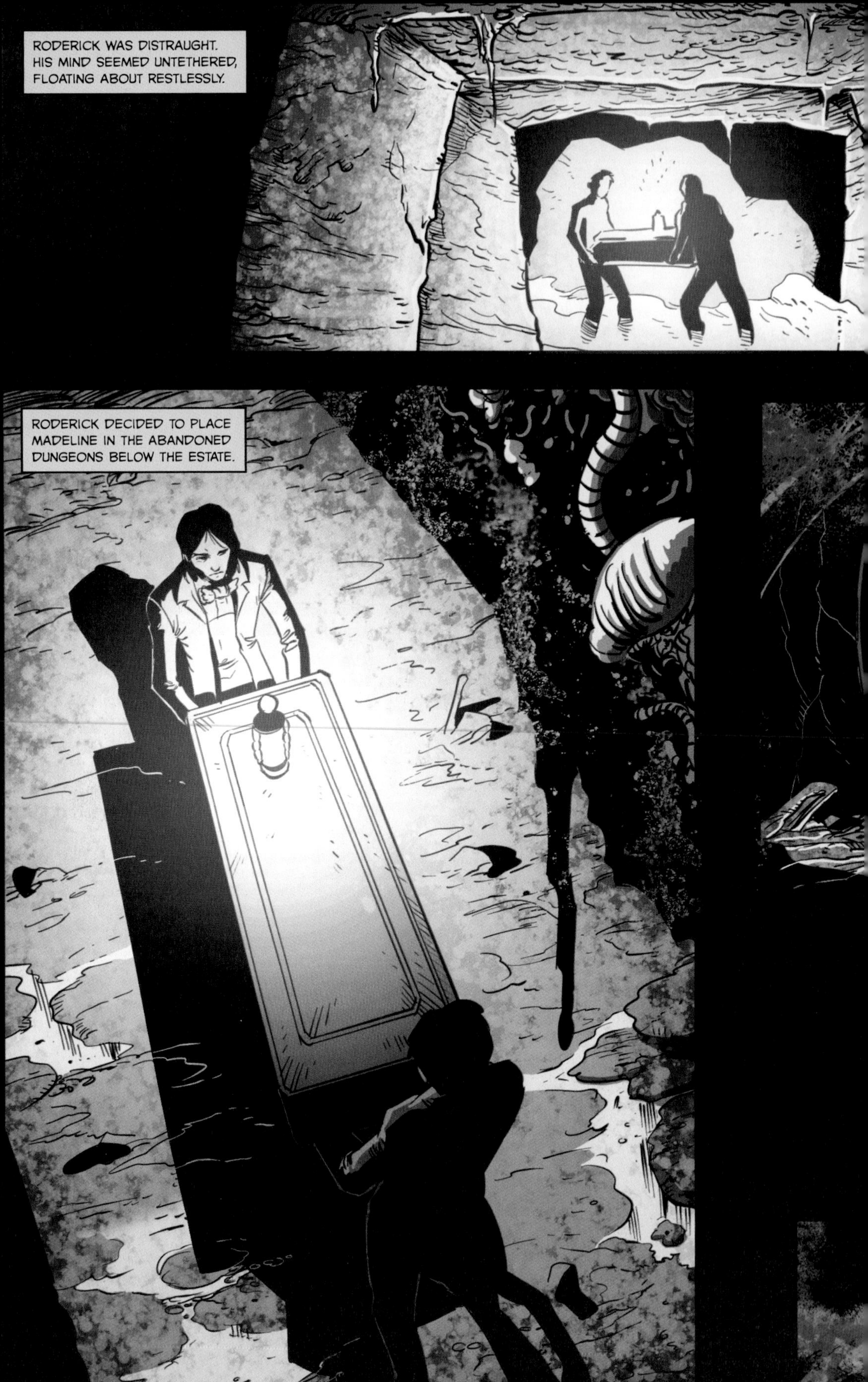
RODERICK WAS DISTRAUGHT. HIS MIND SEEMED UNTETHERED, FLOATING ABOUT RESTLESSLY.
RODERICK DECIDED TO PLACE MADELINE IN THE ABANDONED DUNGEONS BELOW THE ESTATE.

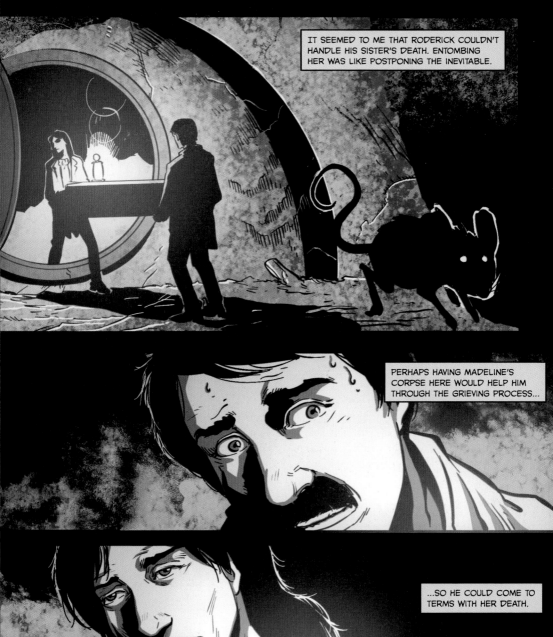

IT SEEMED TO ME THAT RODERICK COULDN'T HANDLE HIS SISTER'S DEATH. ENTOMBING HER WAS LIKE POSTPONING THE INEVITABLE.

PERHAPS HAVING MADELINE'S CORPSE HERE WOULD HELP HIM THROUGH THE GRIEVING PROCESS...

...SO HE COULD COME TO TERMS WITH HER DEATH.

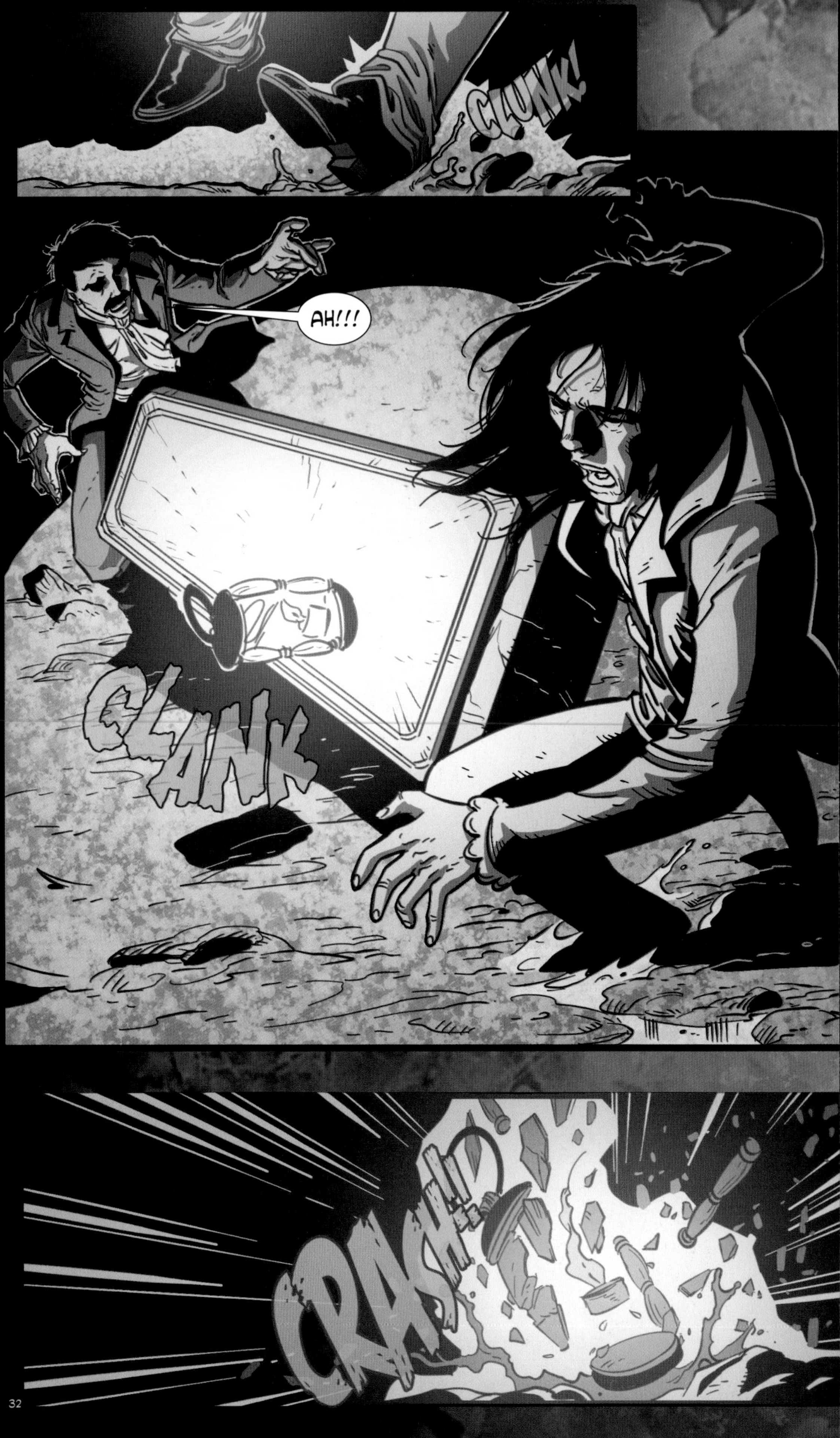
CLUNK!
AH!!!
CLANK
CRASH!

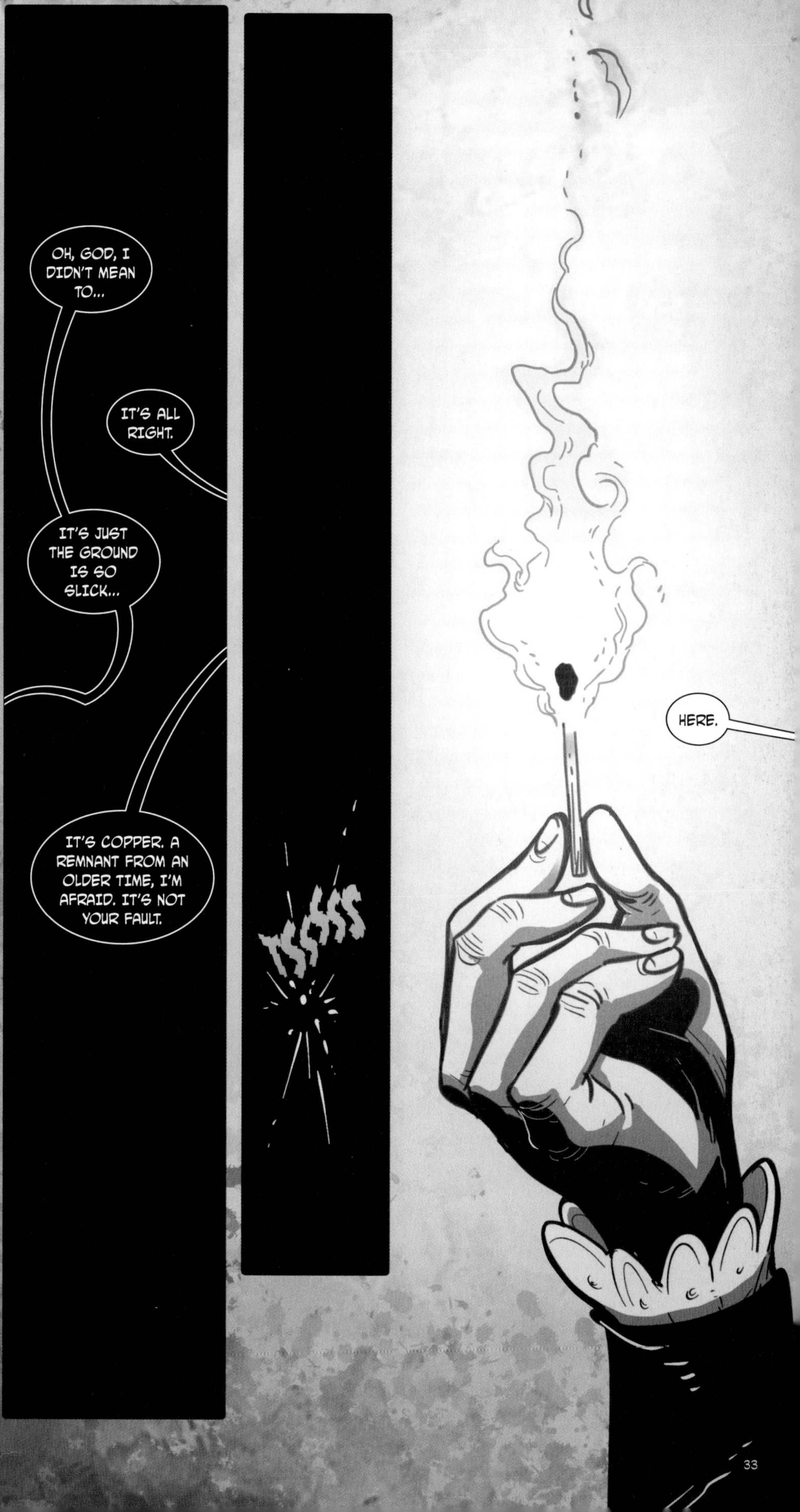
OH, GOD, I DIDN'T MEAN TO...
IT'S ALL RIGHT.
IT'S JUST THE GROUND IS SO SLICK...
IT'S COPPER. A REMNANT FROM AN OLDER TIME, I'M AFRAID. IT'S NOT YOUR FAULT.
TSSSSS
HERE.

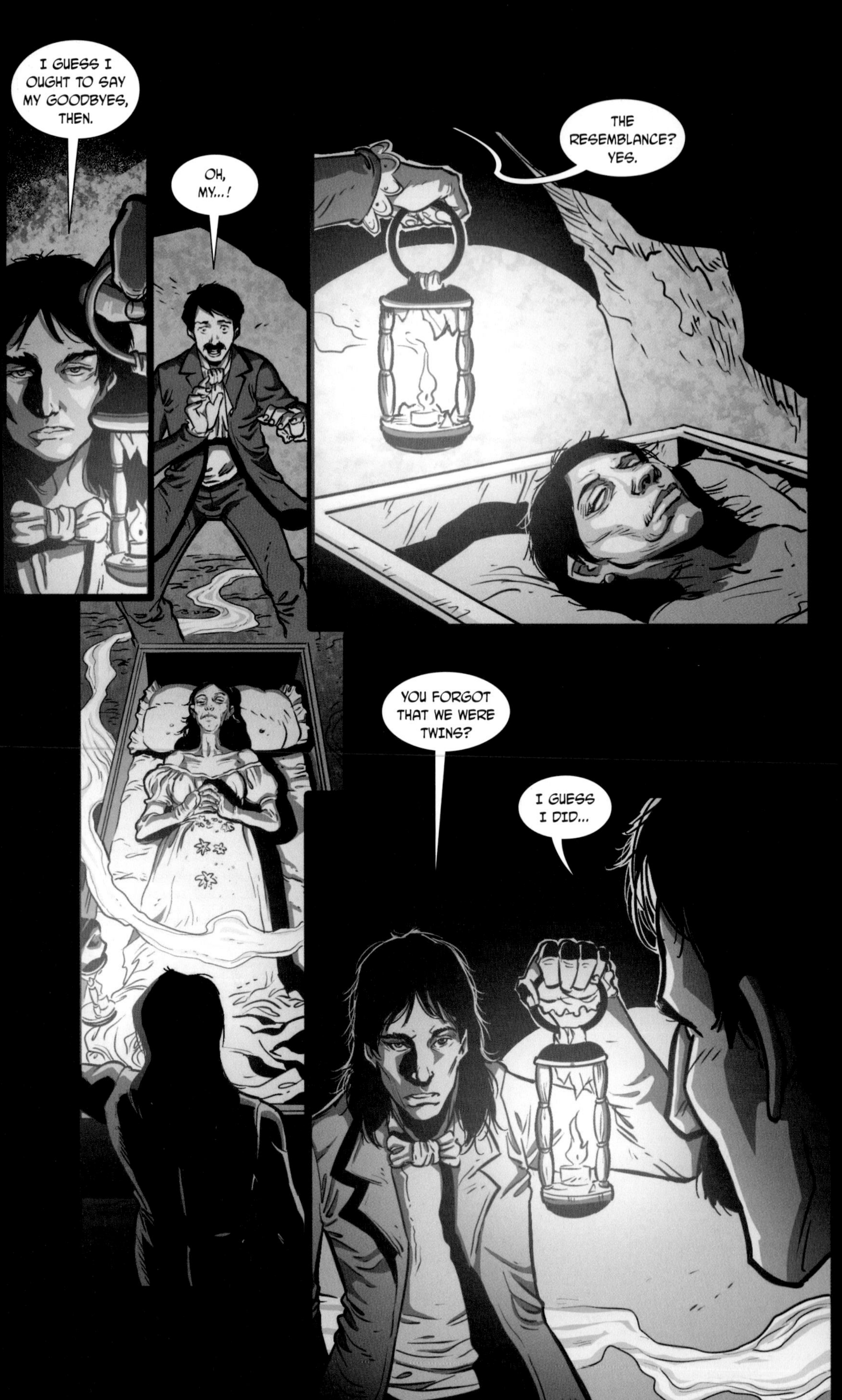
I GUESS I OUGHT TO SAY MY GOODBYES, THEN.
OH, MY...!
THE RESEMBLANCE? YES.
YOU FORGOT THAT WE WERE TWINS?
I GUESS I DID...

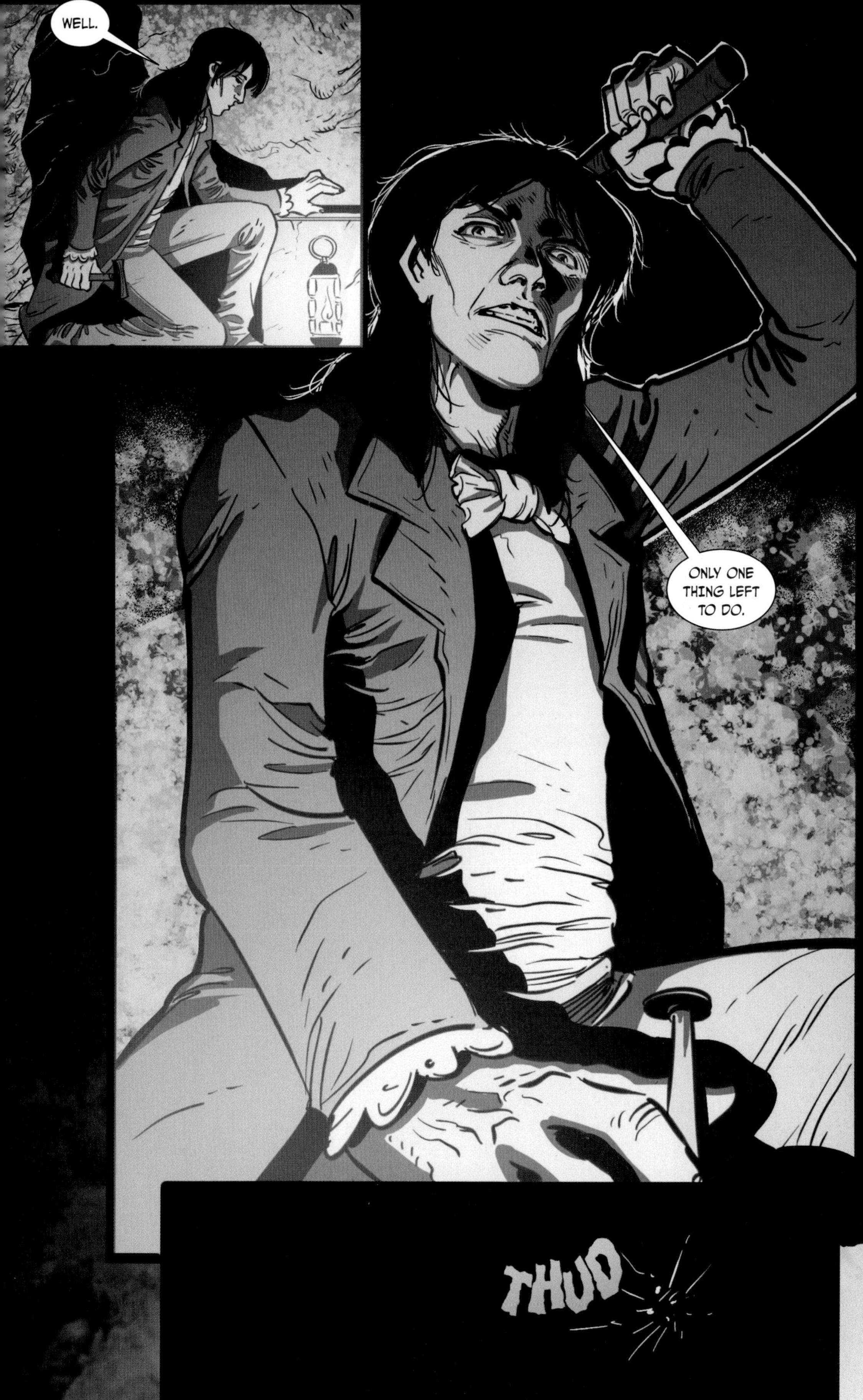
WELL.
ONLY ONE THING LEFT TO DO.
THUD

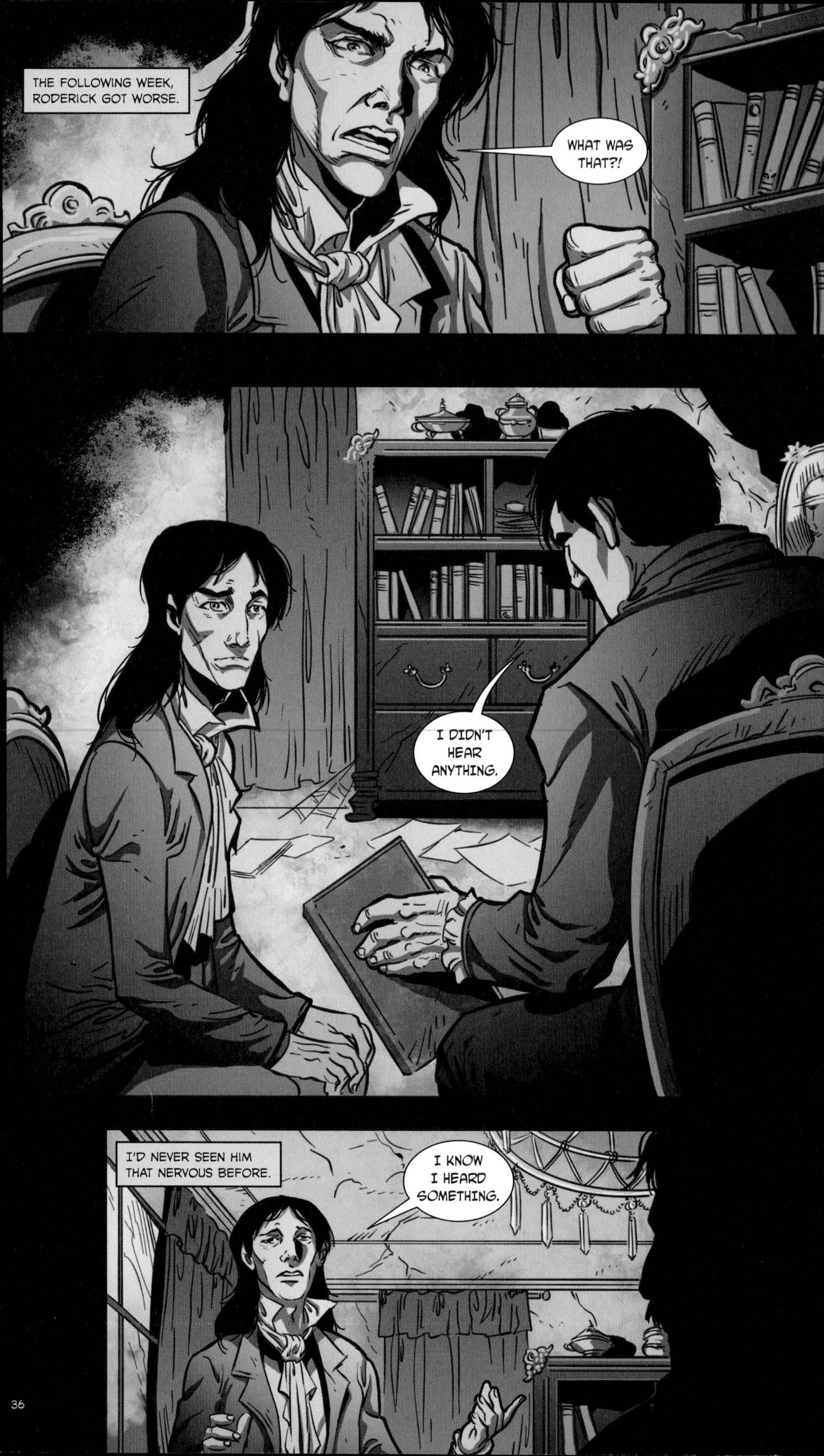
THE FOLLOWING WEEK, RODERICK GOT WORSE.
WHAT WAS THAT?!
I DIDN'T HEAR ANYTHING.
I'D NEVER SEEN HIM THAT NERVOUS BEFORE.
I KNOW I HEARD SOMETHING.

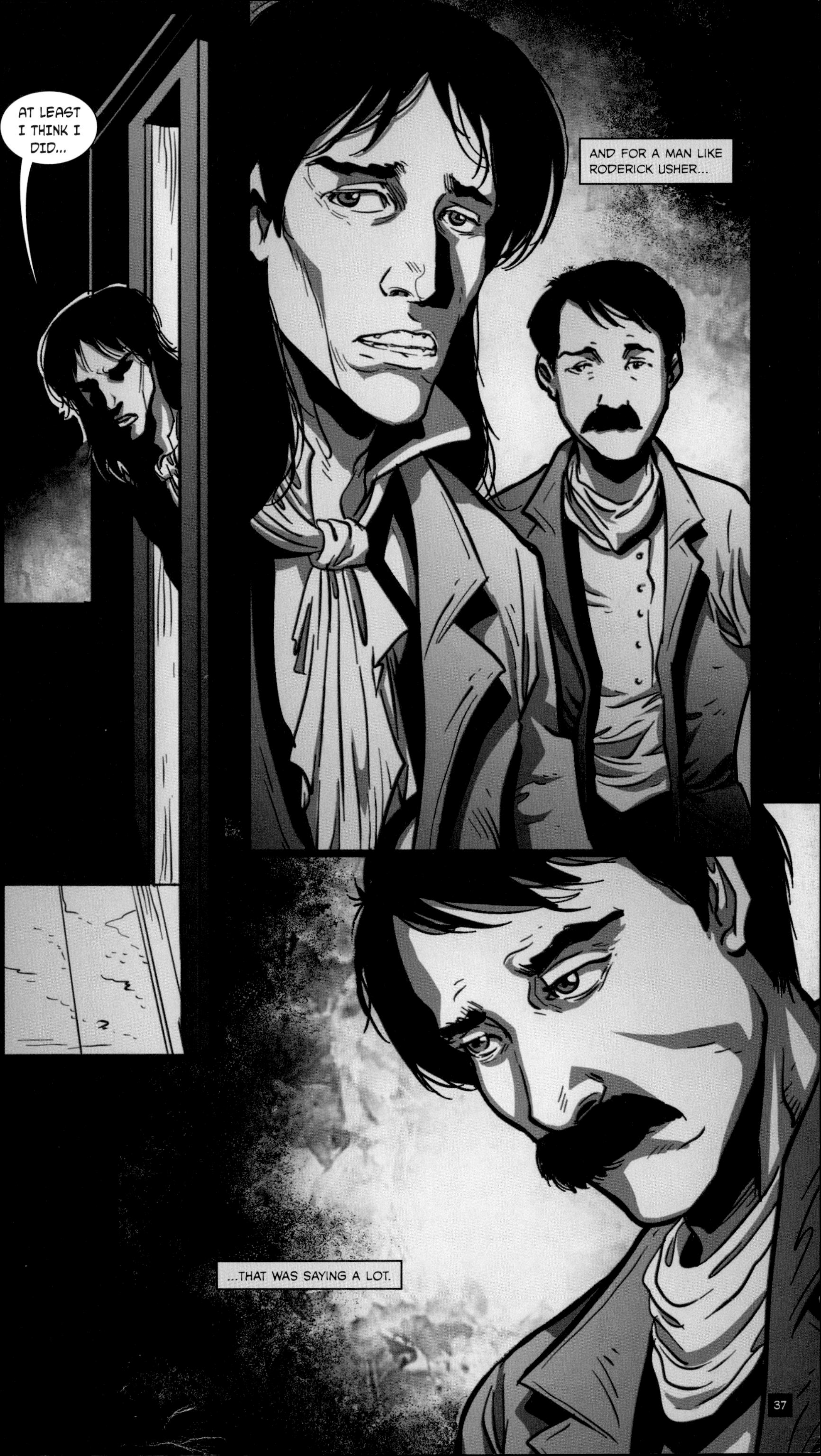

AT LEAST I THINK I DID...
AND FOR A MAN LIKE RODERICK USHER...
...THAT WAS SAYING A LOT.

THERE WAS NO REST FOR RODERICK THAT WEEK.

WOOSH!

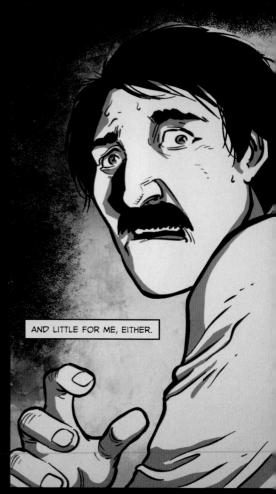

AND LITTLE FOR ME, EITHER.

I KEPT HEARING NOISES.

THUMP!

THUMP!

OOOOOOO

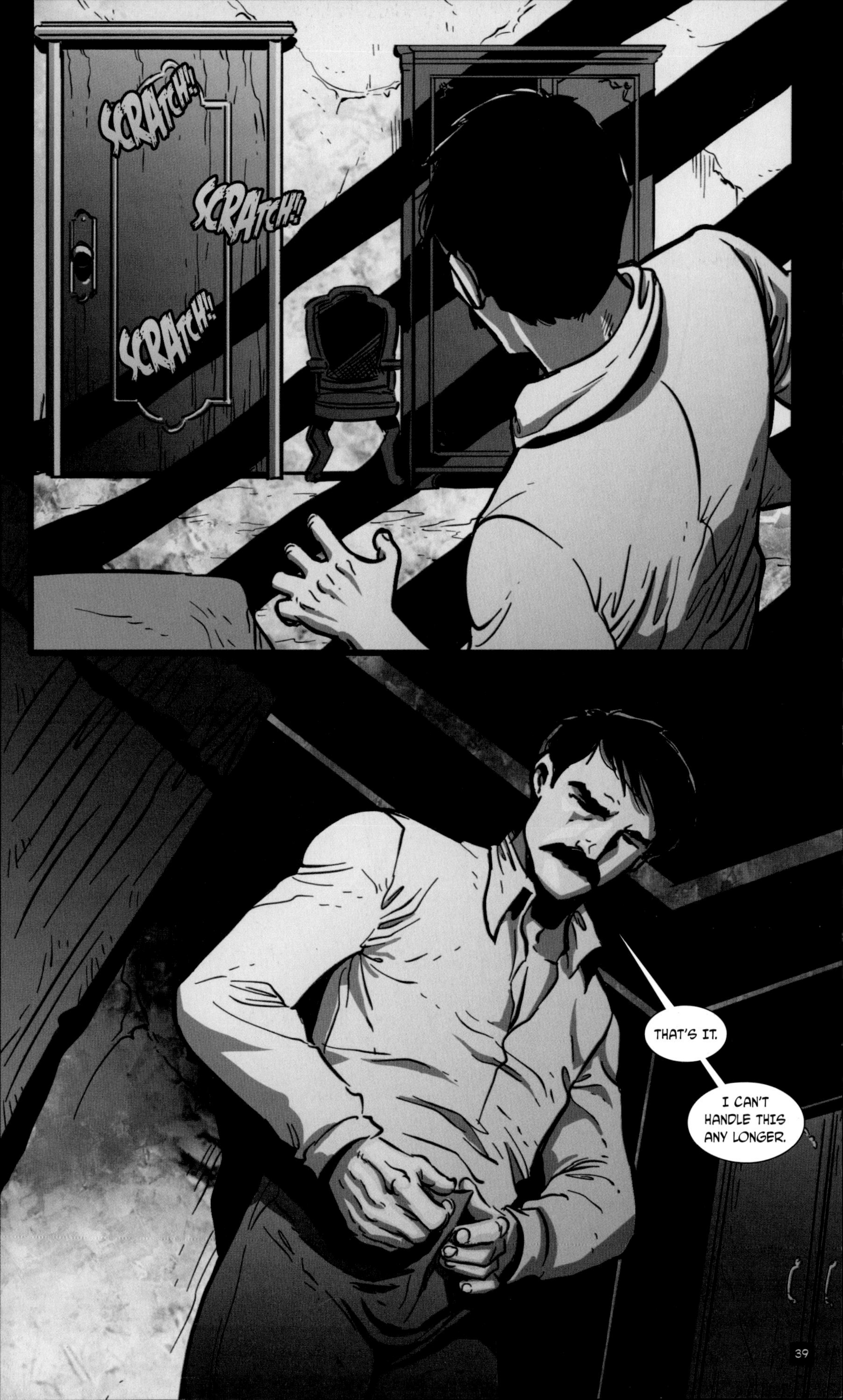
SCRATCH!!
SCRATCH!!
SCRATCH!!
THAT'S IT.
I CAN'T HANDLE THIS ANY LONGER.

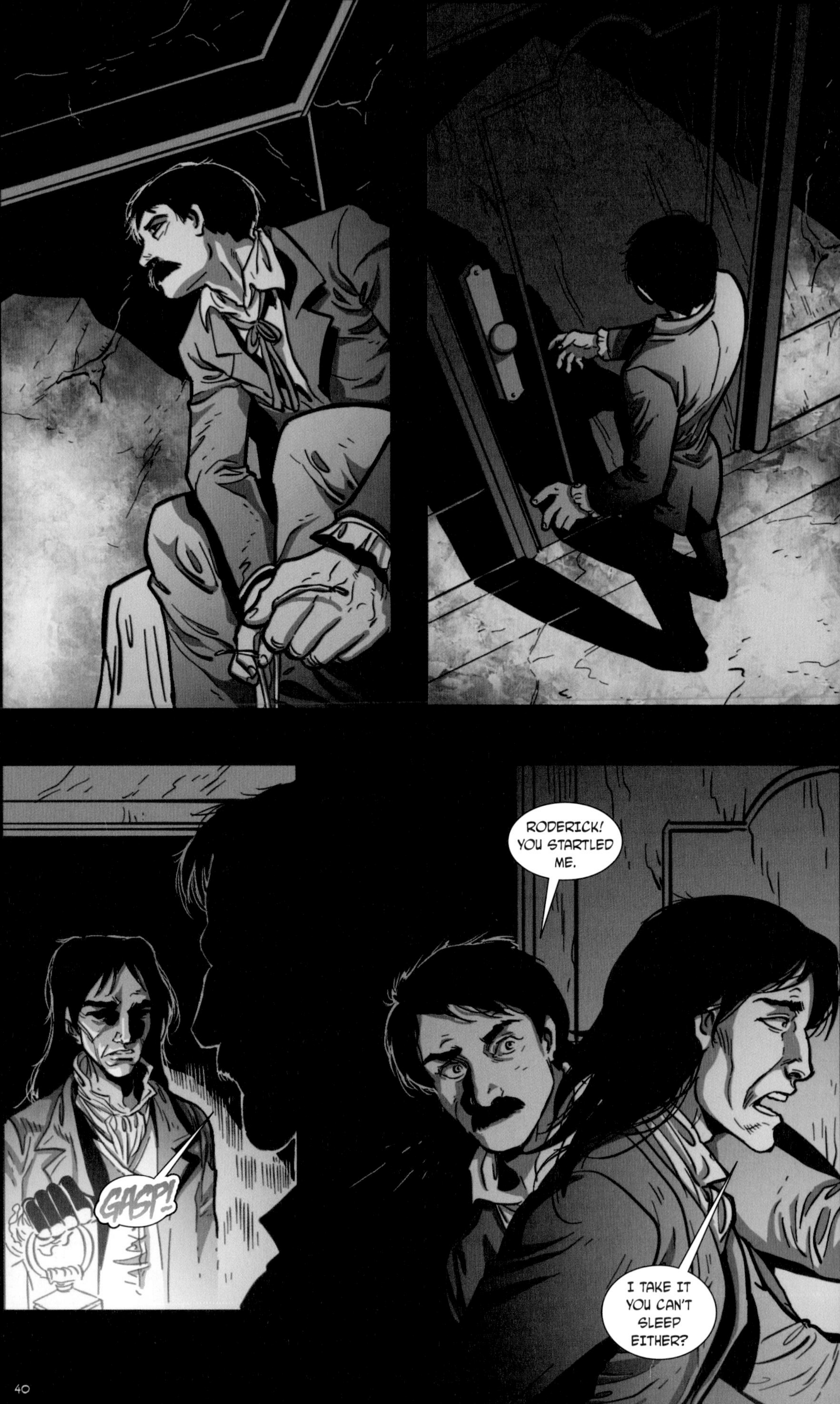
GASP!
RODERICK! YOU STARTLED ME.
I TAKE IT YOU CAN'T SLEEP EITHER?

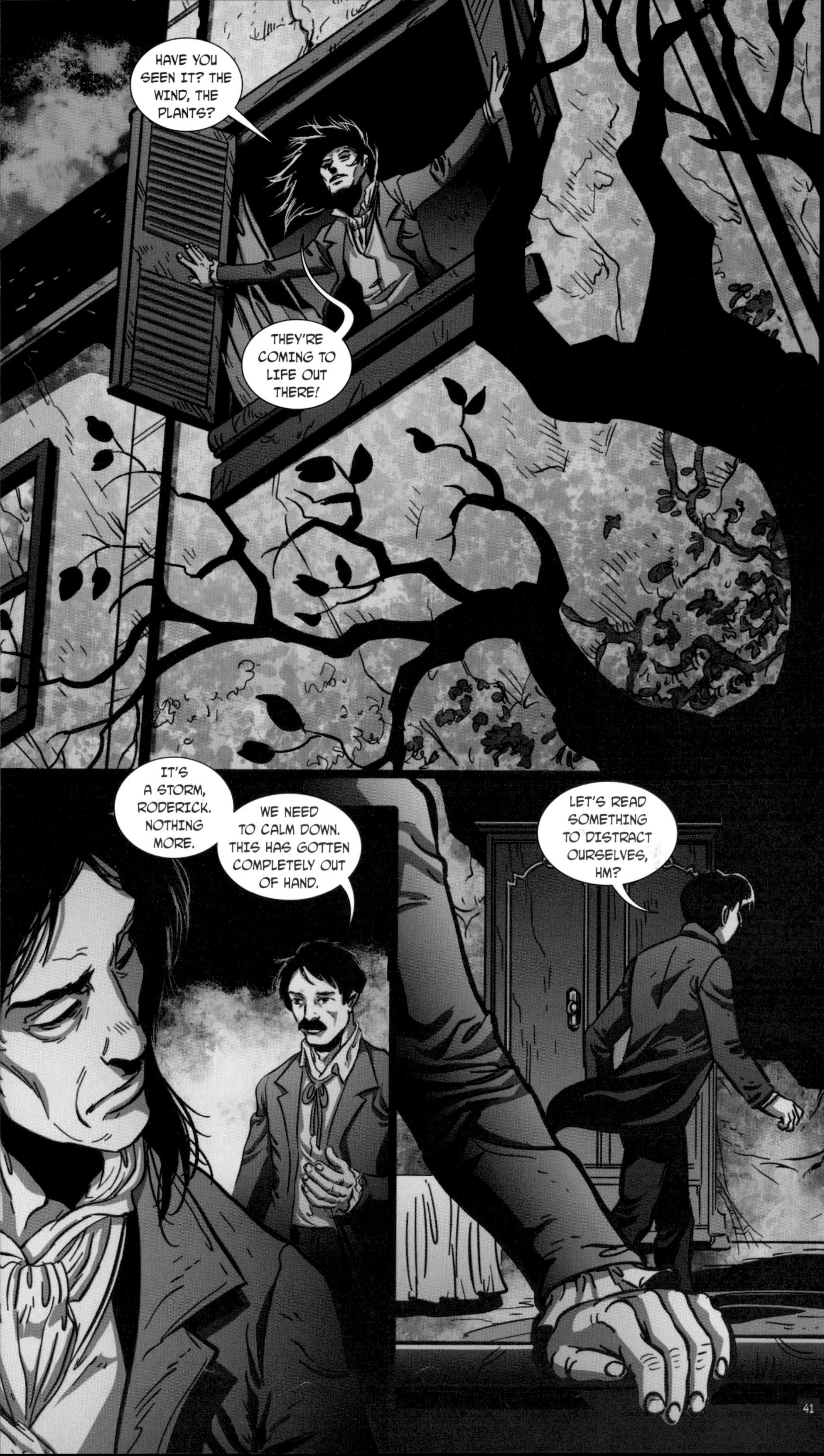
HAVE YOU SEEN IT? THE WIND, THE PLANTS?
THEY'RE COMING TO LIFE OUT THERE!
IT'S A STORM, RODERICK. NOTHING MORE.
WE NEED TO CALM DOWN. THIS HAS GOTTEN COMPLETELY OUT OF HAND.
LET'S READ SOMETHING TO DISTRACT OURSELVES, HM?

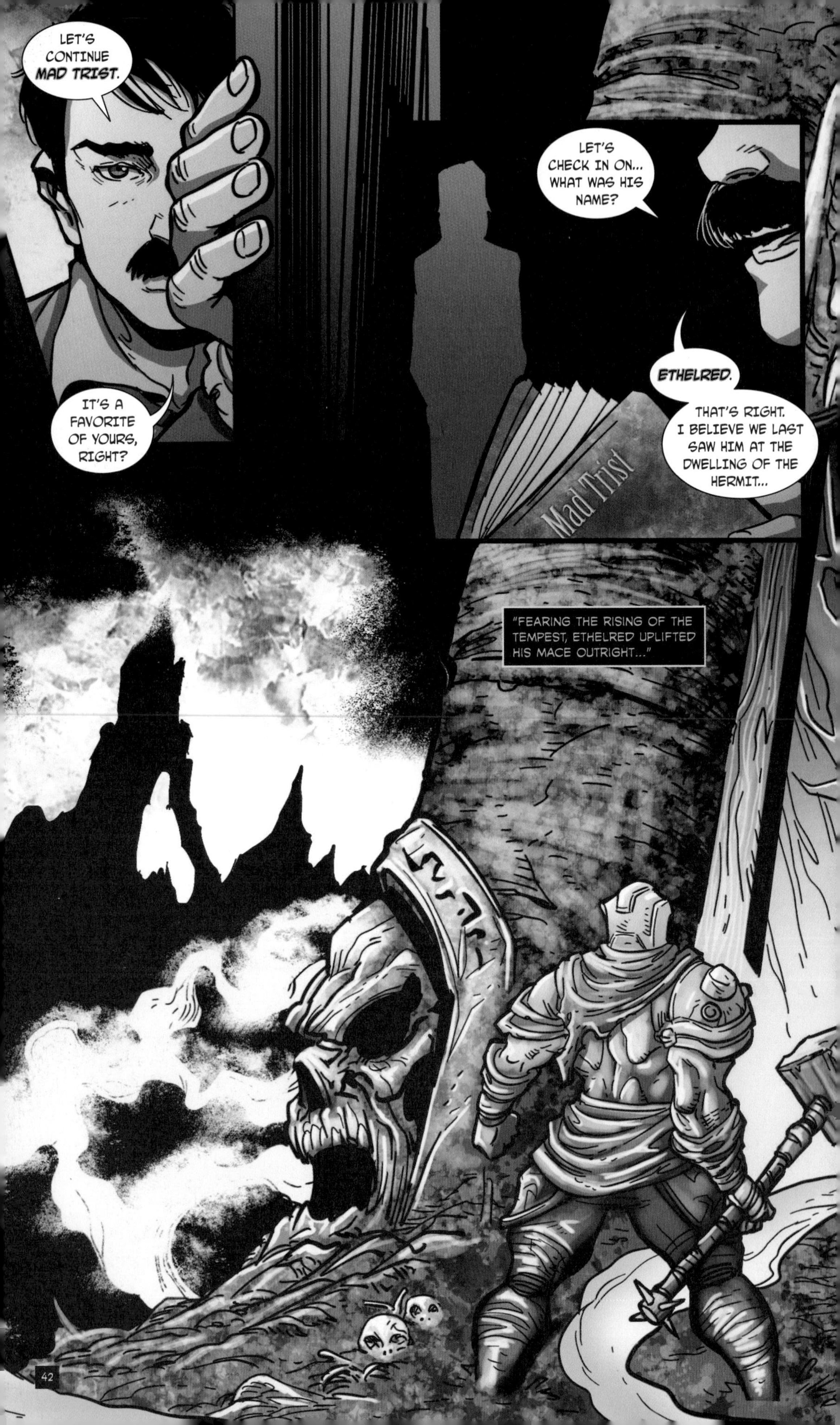

LET'S CONTINUE ***MAD TRIST.***
IT'S A FAVORITE OF YOURS, RIGHT?
LET'S CHECK IN ON... WHAT WAS HIS NAME?
ETHELRED.
THAT'S RIGHT. I BELIEVE WE LAST SAW HIM AT THE DWELLING OF THE HERMIT...
Mad Trist
"FEARING THE RISING OF THE TEMPEST, ETHELRED UPLIFTED HIS MACE OUTRIGHT..."

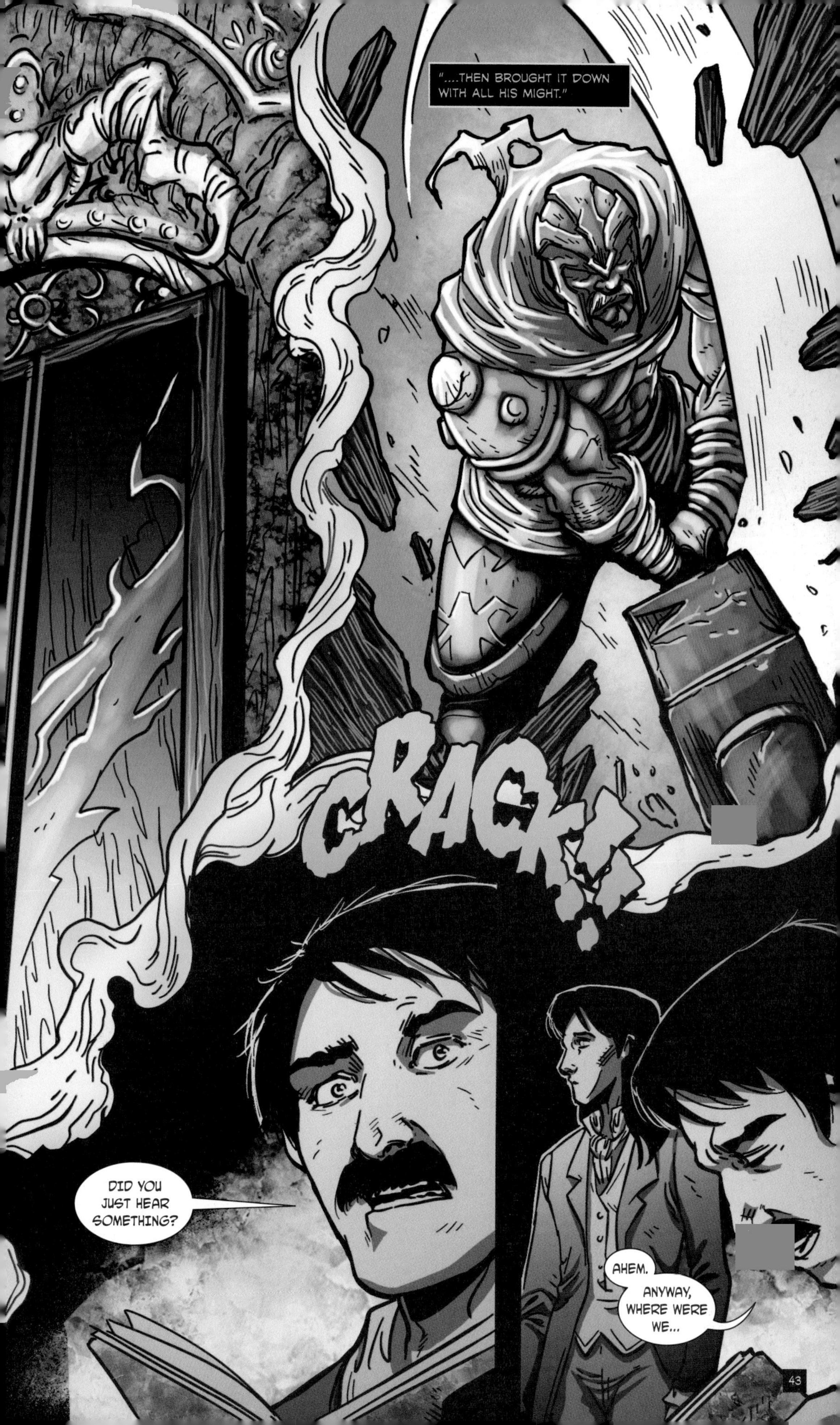

"....THEN BROUGHT IT DOWN WITH ALL HIS MIGHT."
CRACK!!
DID YOU JUST HEAR SOMETHING?
AHEM.
ANYWAY, WHERE WERE WE...

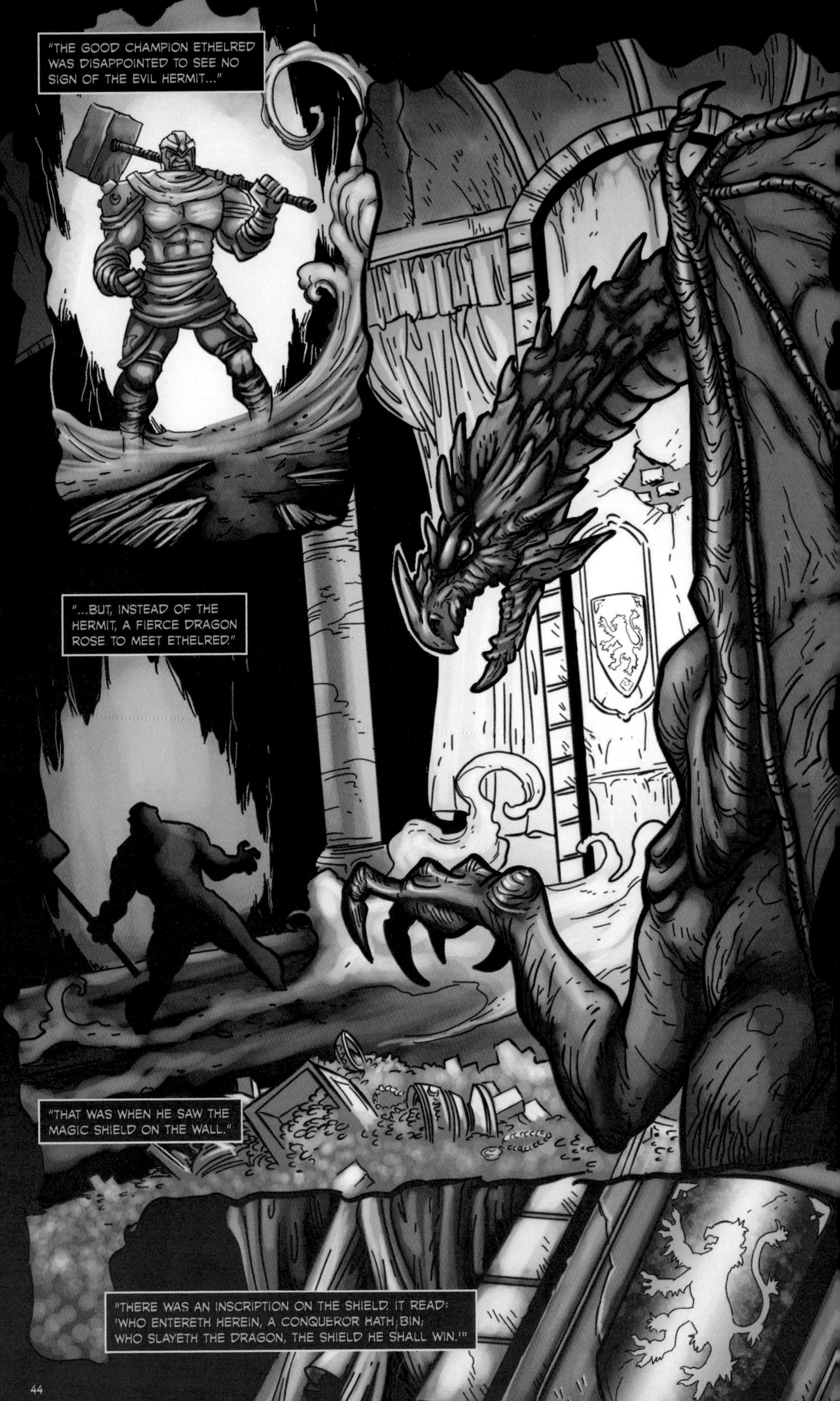
"THE GOOD CHAMPION ETHELRED WAS DISAPPOINTED TO SEE NO SIGN OF THE EVIL HERMIT..."
"...BUT, INSTEAD OF THE HERMIT, A FIERCE DRAGON ROSE TO MEET ETHELRED."
"THAT WAS WHEN HE SAW THE MAGIC SHIELD ON THE WALL."
"THERE WAS AN INSCRIPTION ON THE SHIELD. IT READ: 'WHO ENTERETH HEREIN, A CONQUEROR HATH BIN; WHO SLAYETH THE DRAGON, THE SHIELD HE SHALL WIN.'"

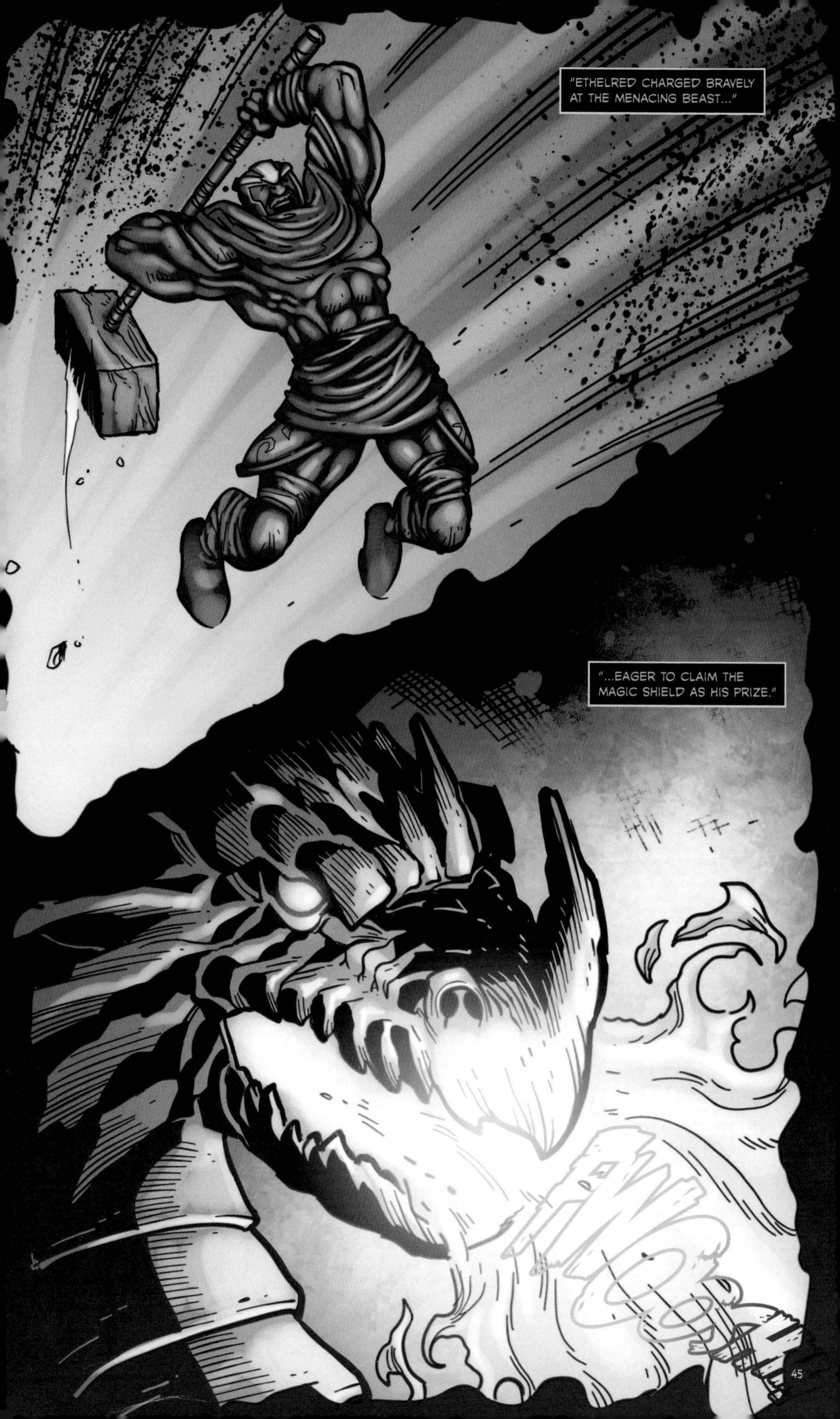
"ETHELRED CHARGED BRAVELY AT THE MENACING BEAST..."
"...EAGER TO CLAIM THE MAGIC SHIELD AS HIS PRIZE."

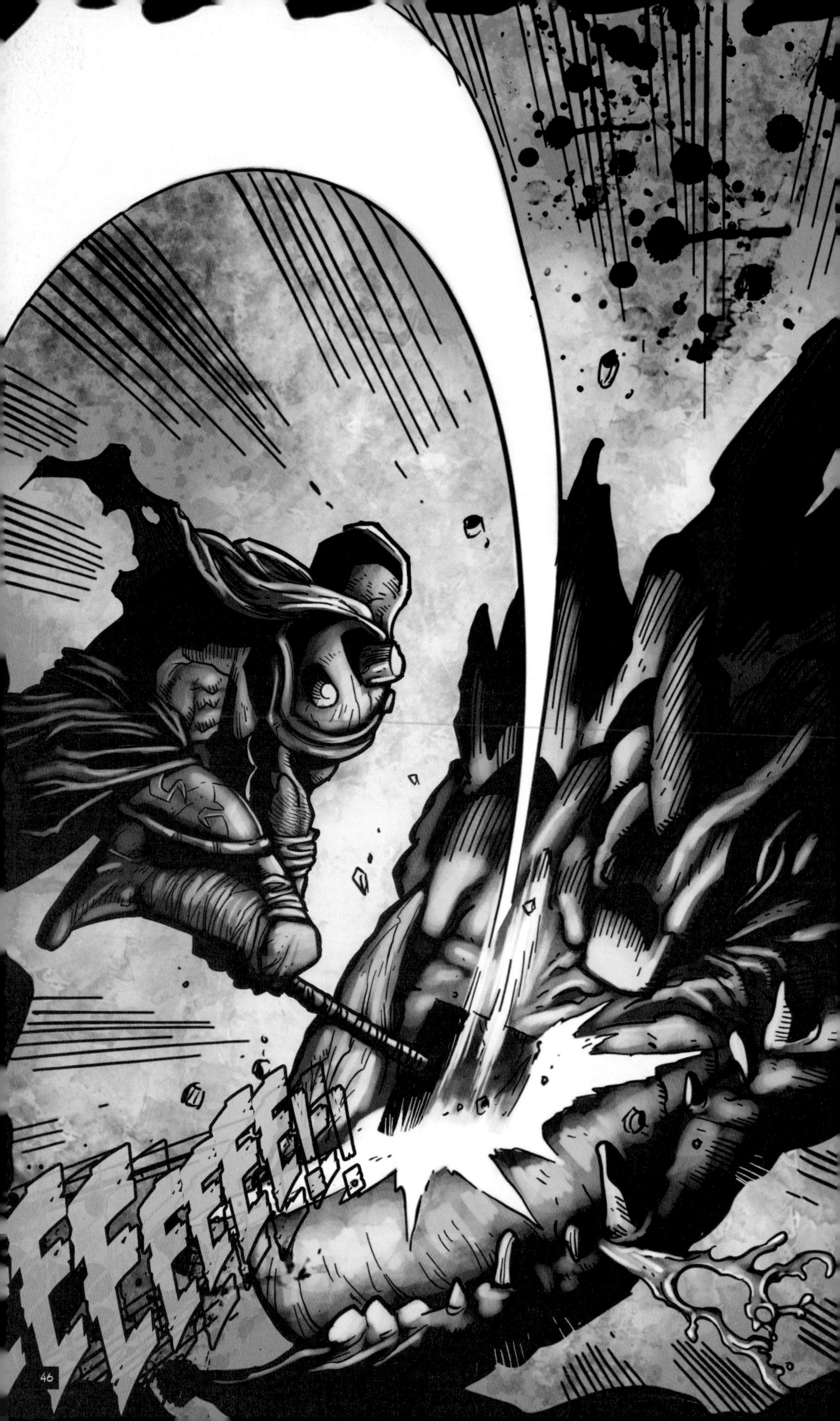
EEEEEEE!!

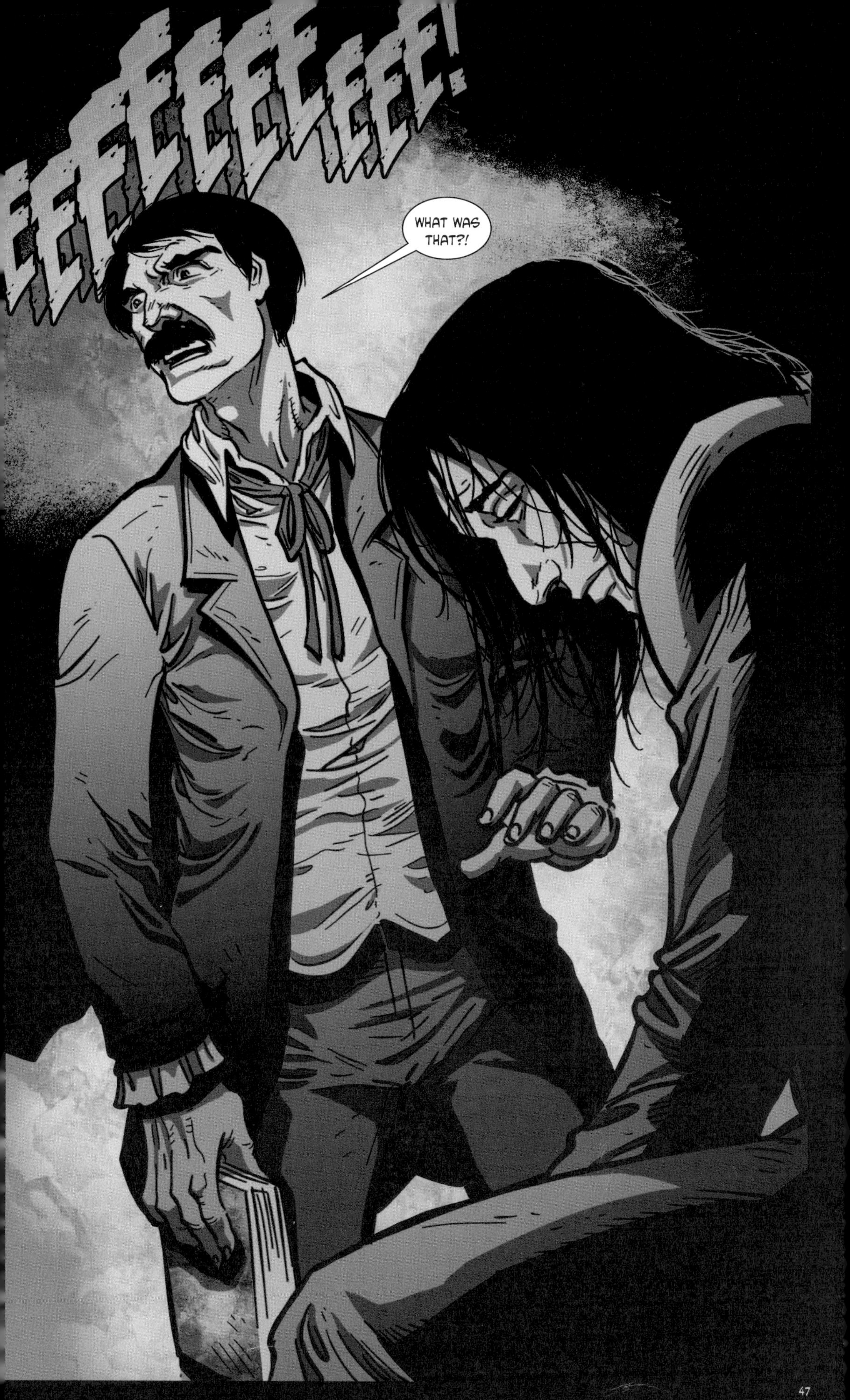
EEEEEEEEEEEEE!
WHAT WAS THAT?!

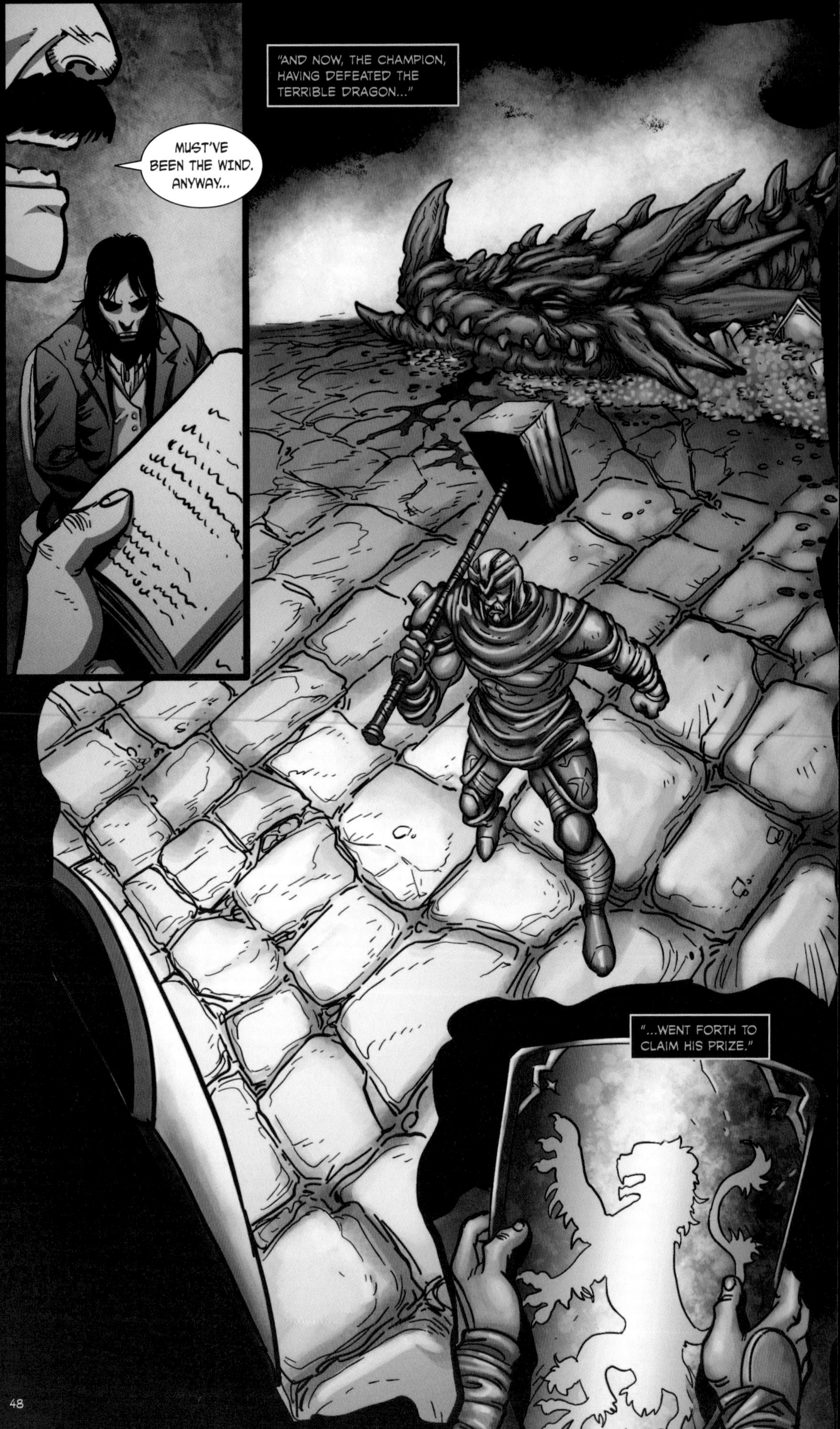

MUST'VE BEEN THE WIND. ANYWAY...
"AND NOW, THE CHAMPION, HAVING DEFEATED THE TERRIBLE DRAGON..."
"...WENT FORTH TO CLAIM HIS PRIZE."

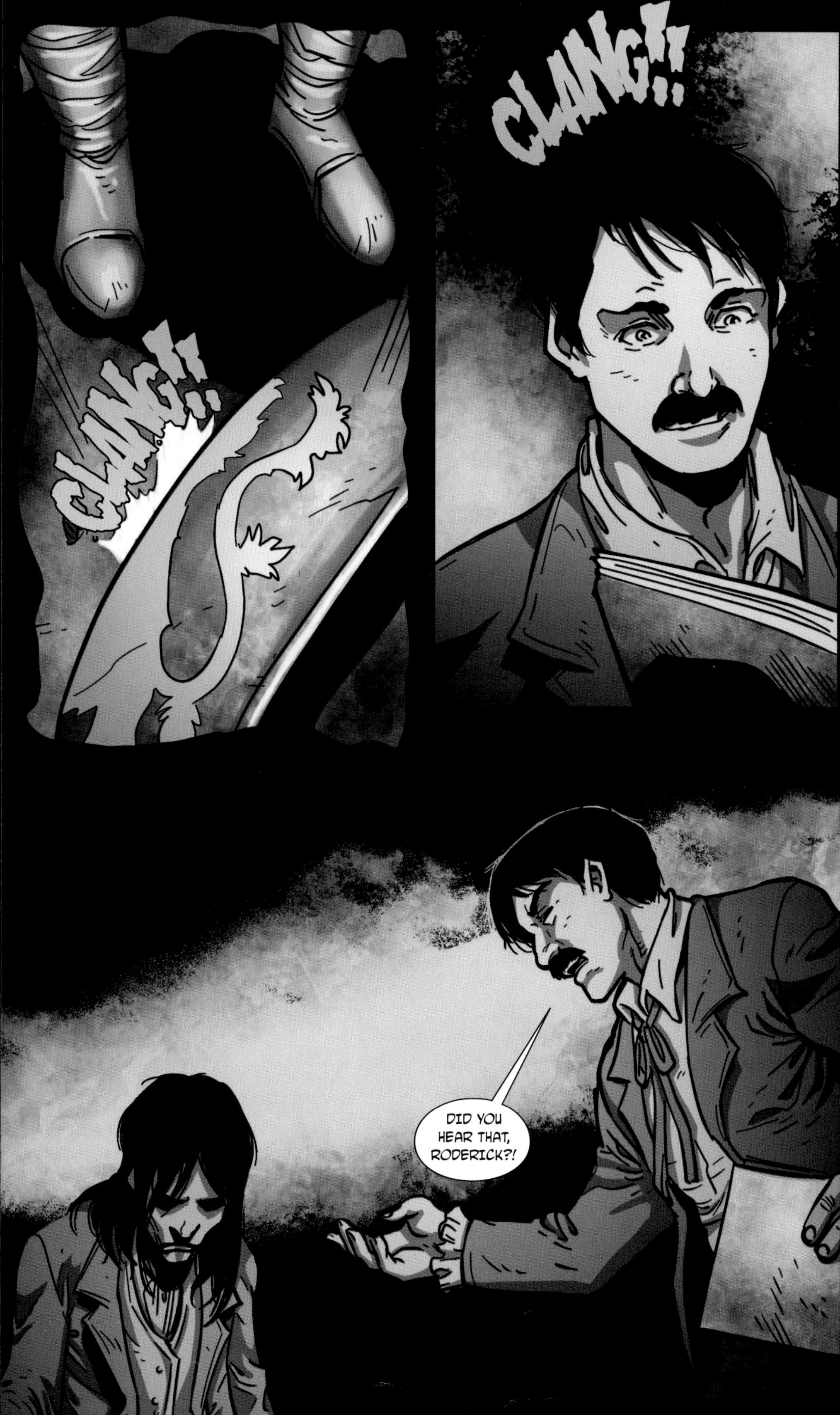
CLANG!!
CLANG!!
DID YOU HEAR THAT, RODERICK?!

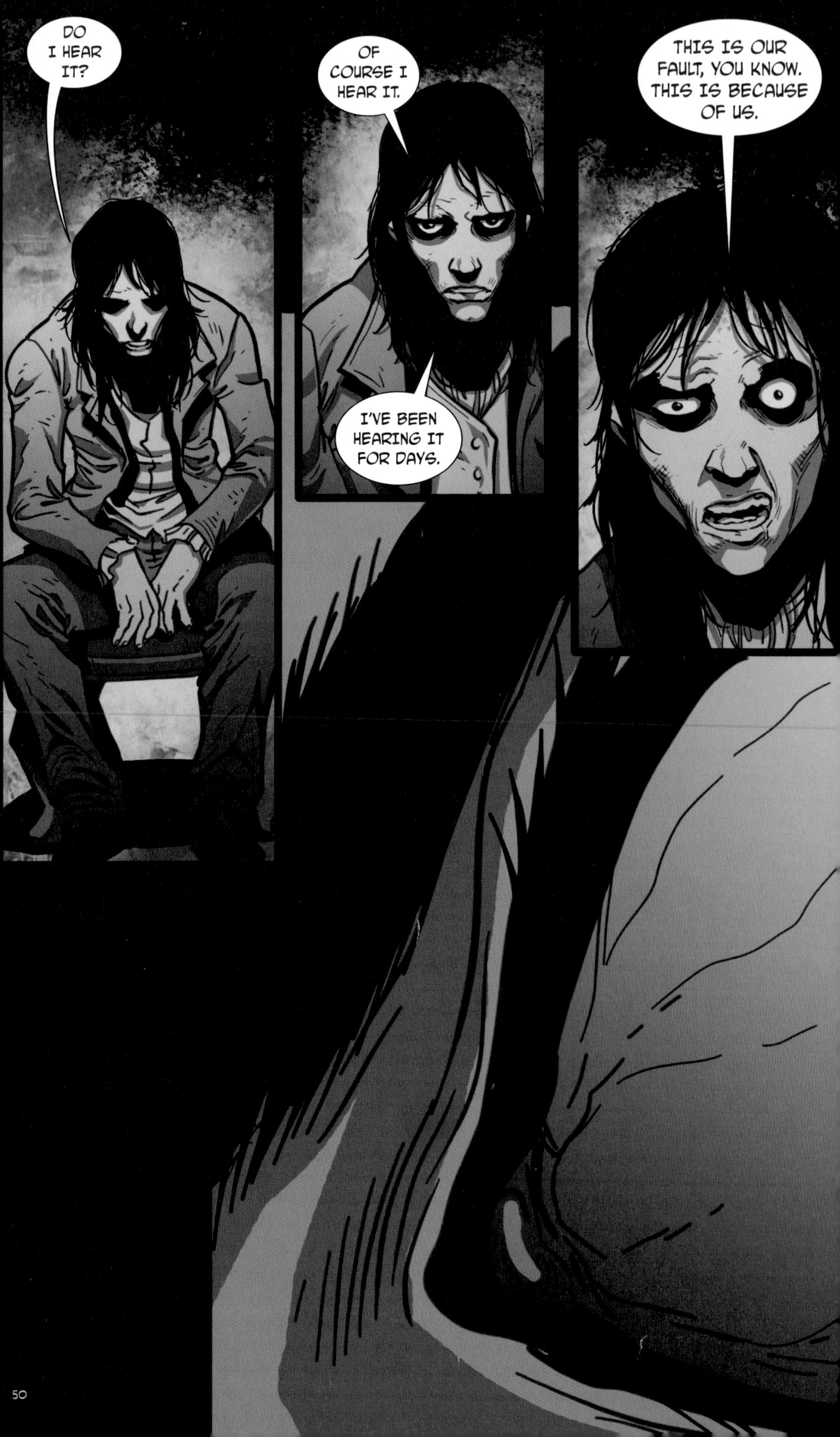
DO I HEAR IT?
OF COURSE I HEAR IT.
I'VE BEEN HEARING IT FOR DAYS.
THIS IS OUR FAULT, YOU KNOW. THIS IS BECAUSE OF US.

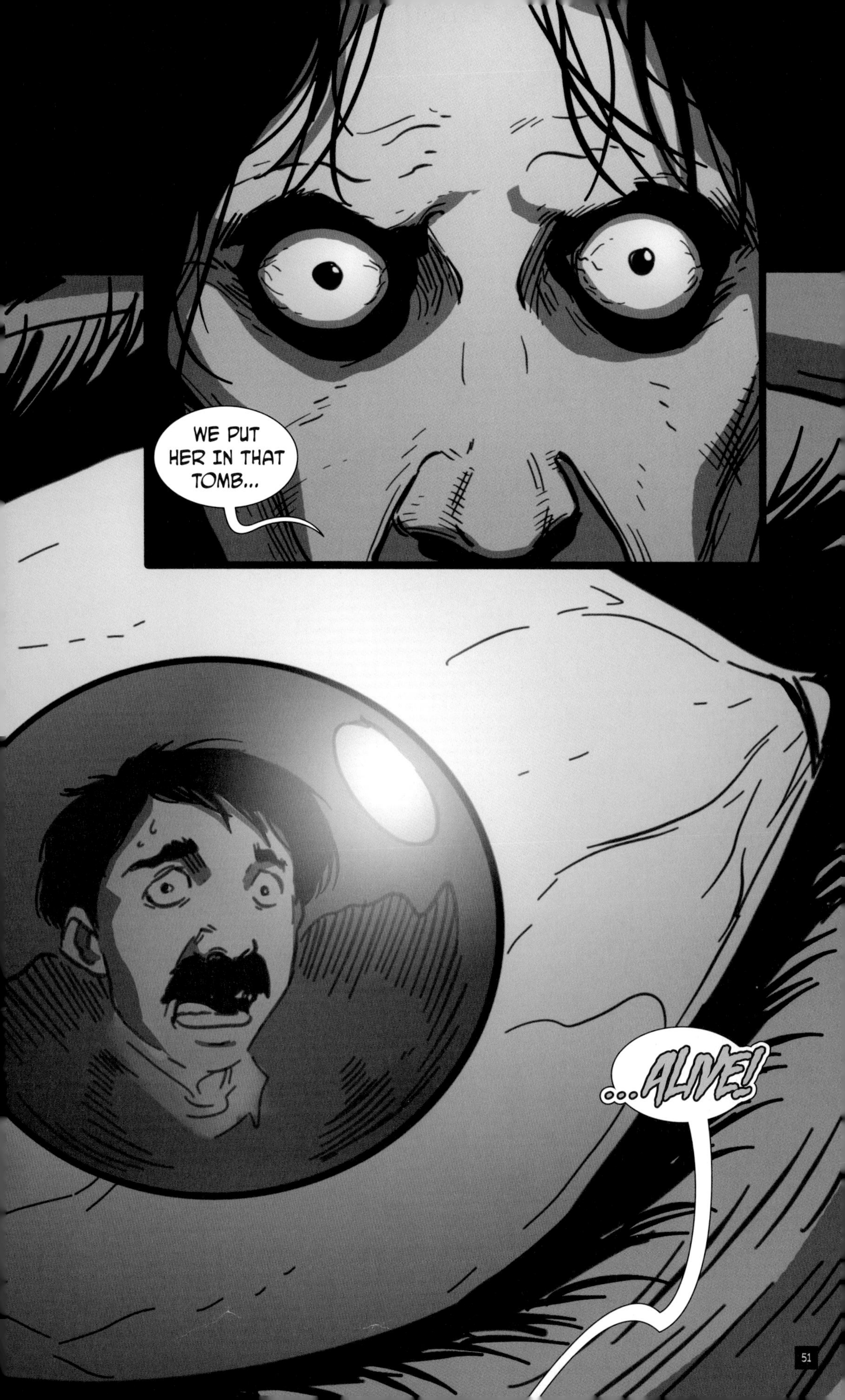
WE PUT HER IN THAT TOMB...
...ALIVE!

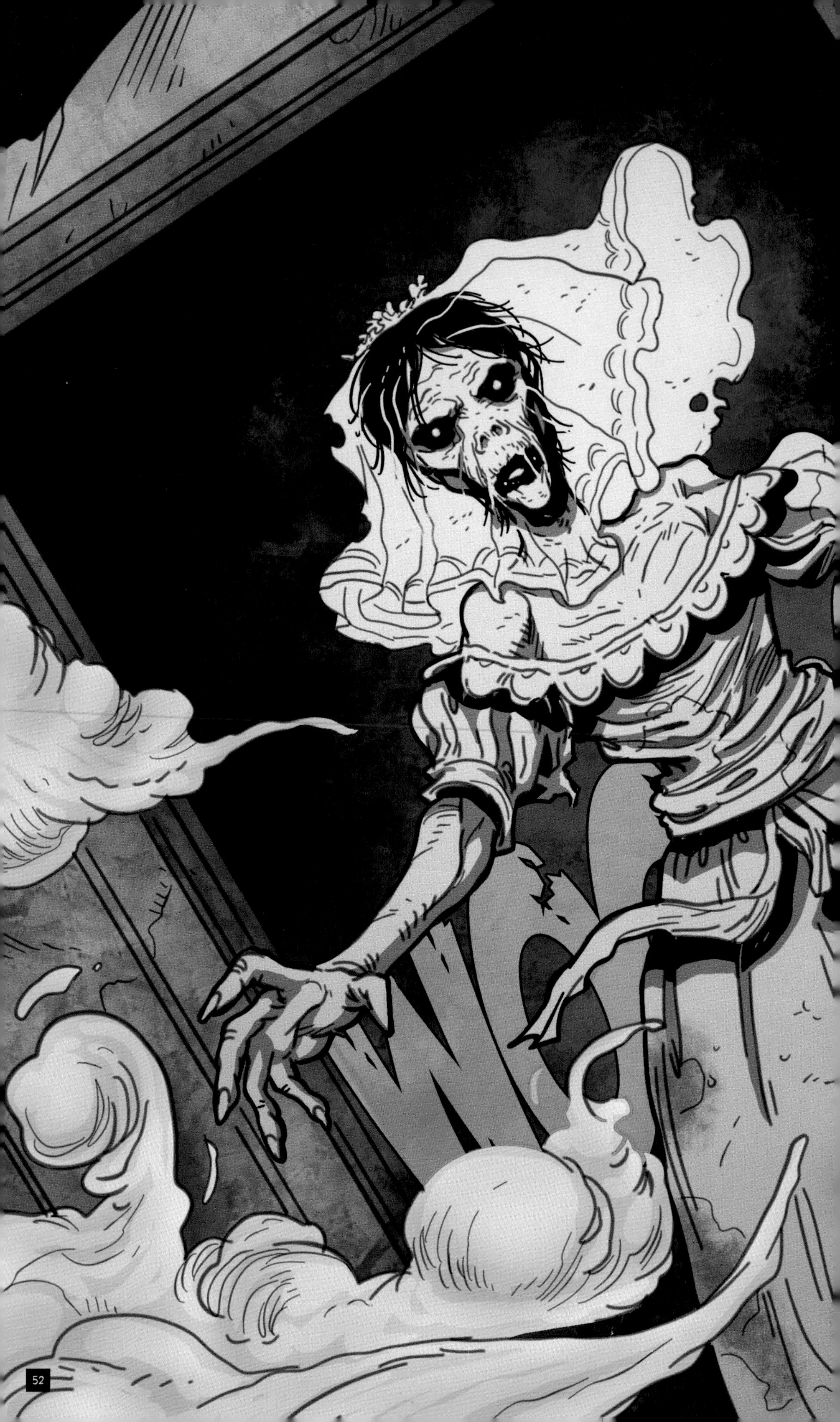

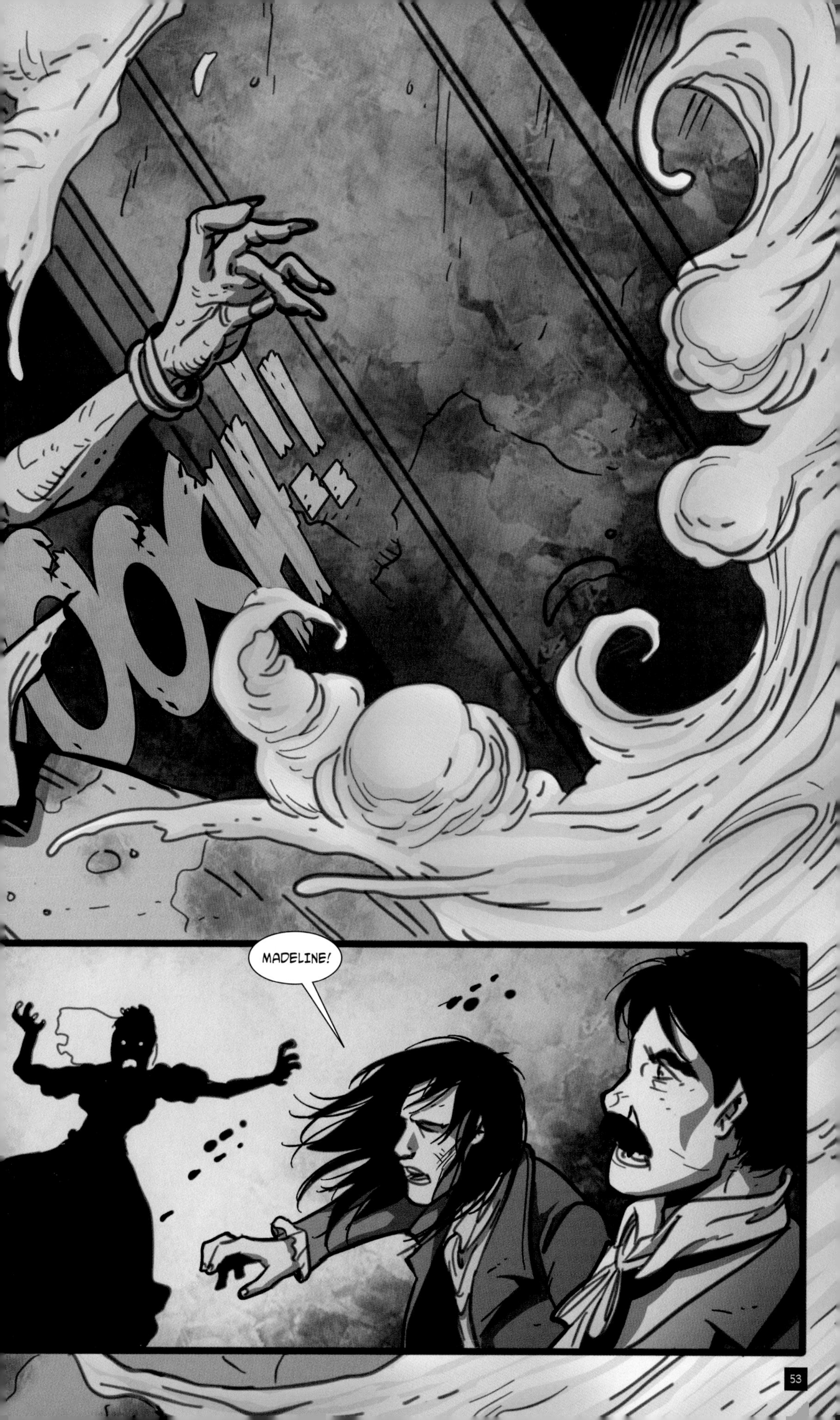
MADELINE!

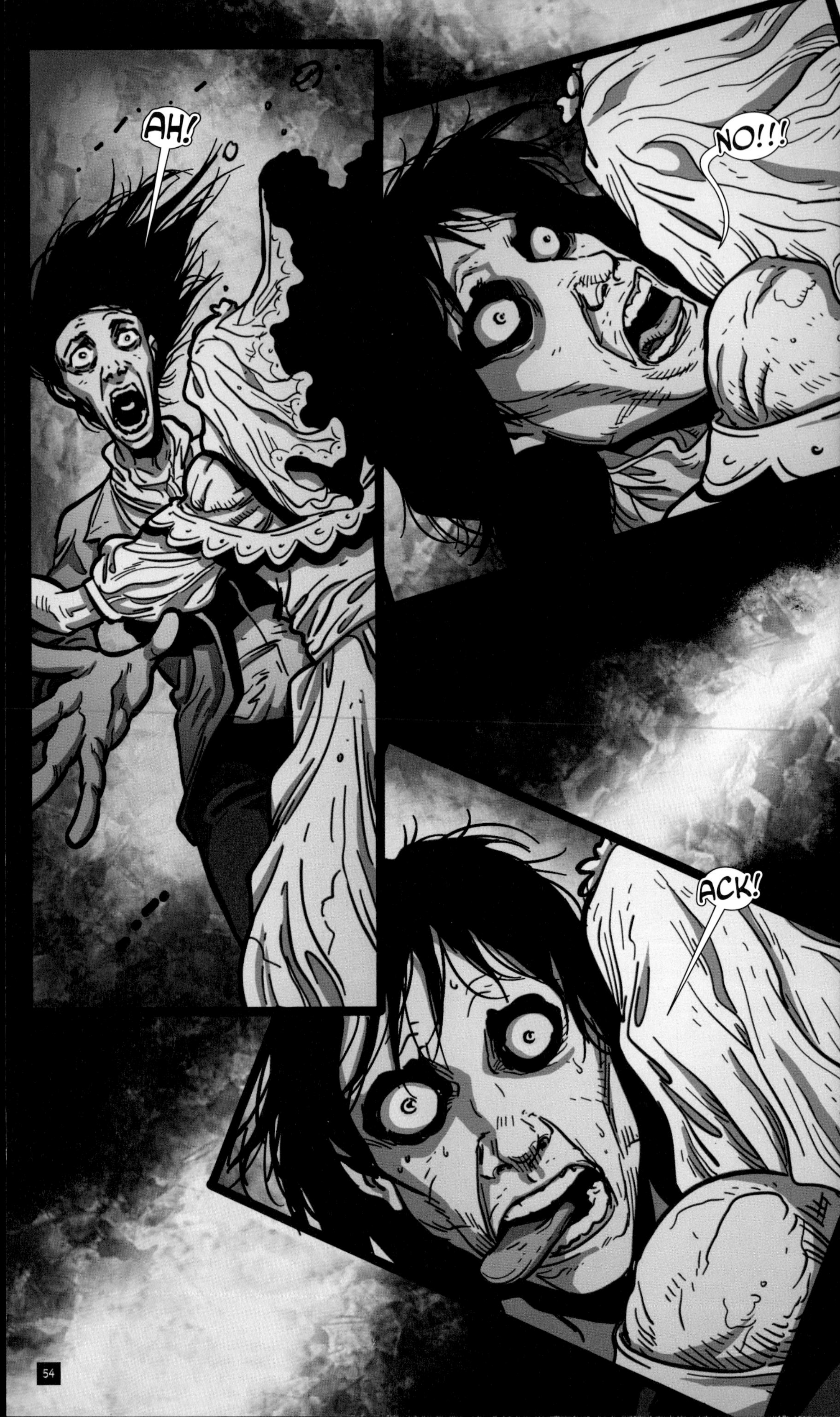
AH!
NO!!!
ACK!

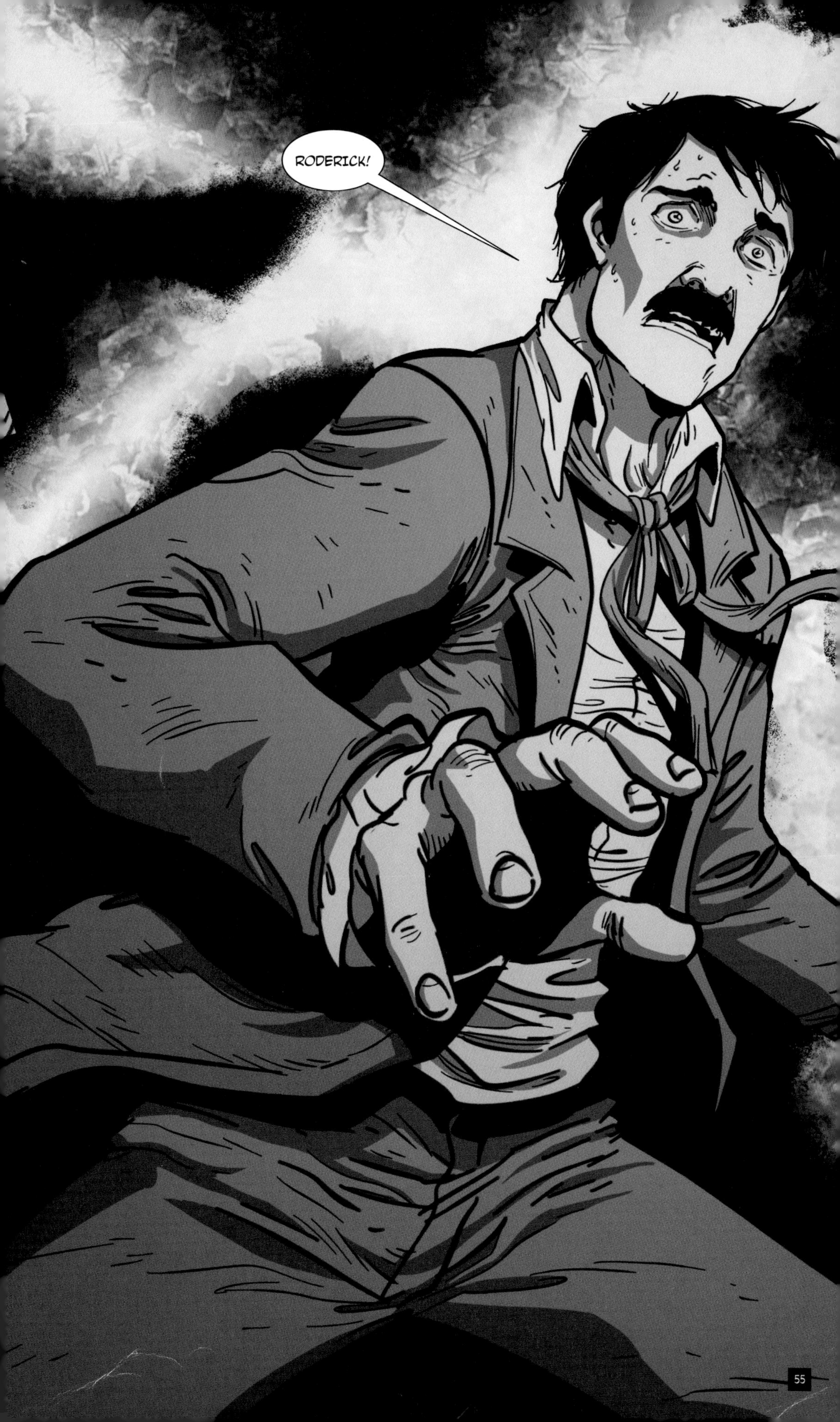
RODERICK!

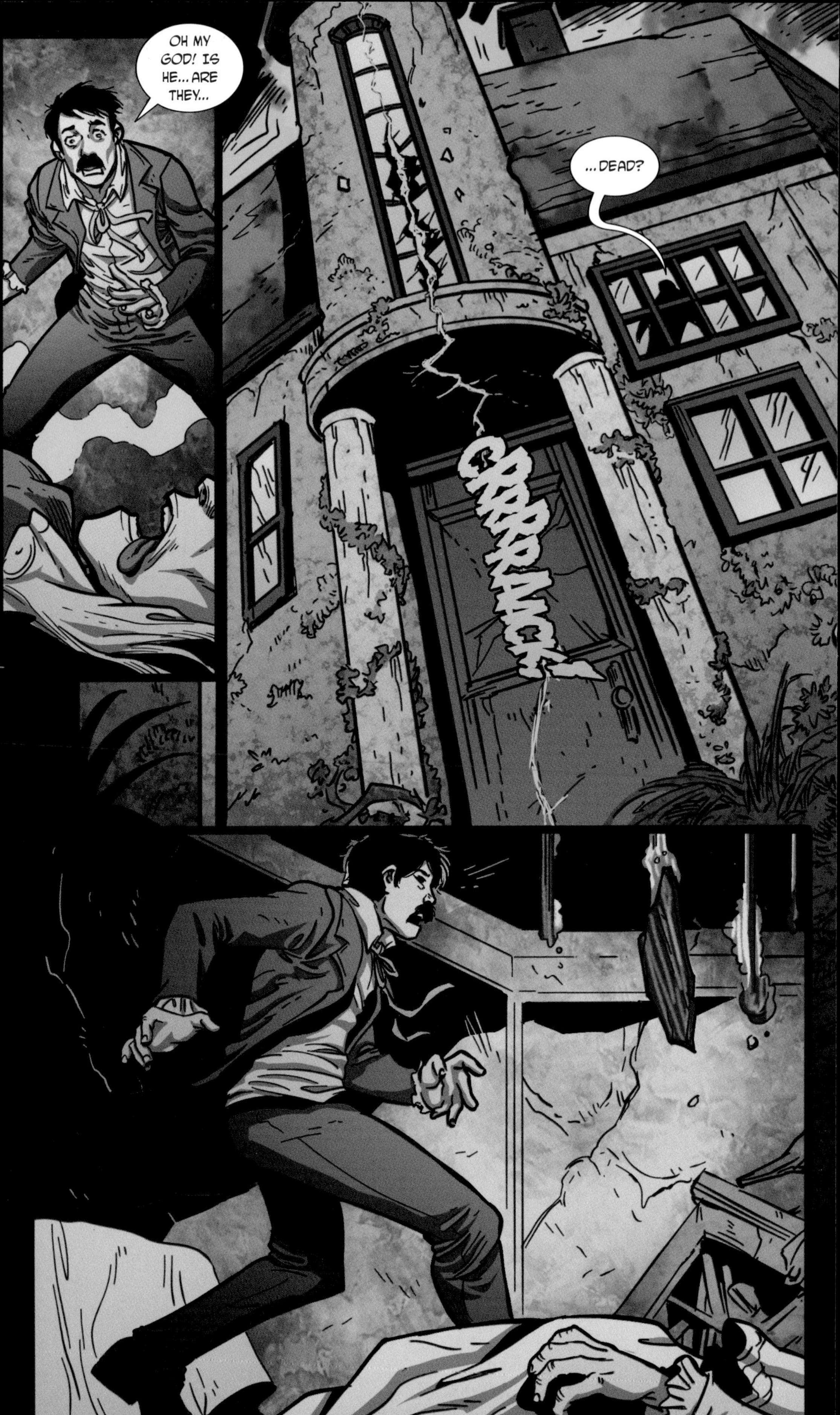
OH MY GOD! IS HE... ARE THEY...
...DEAD?
CRRRRAACK!

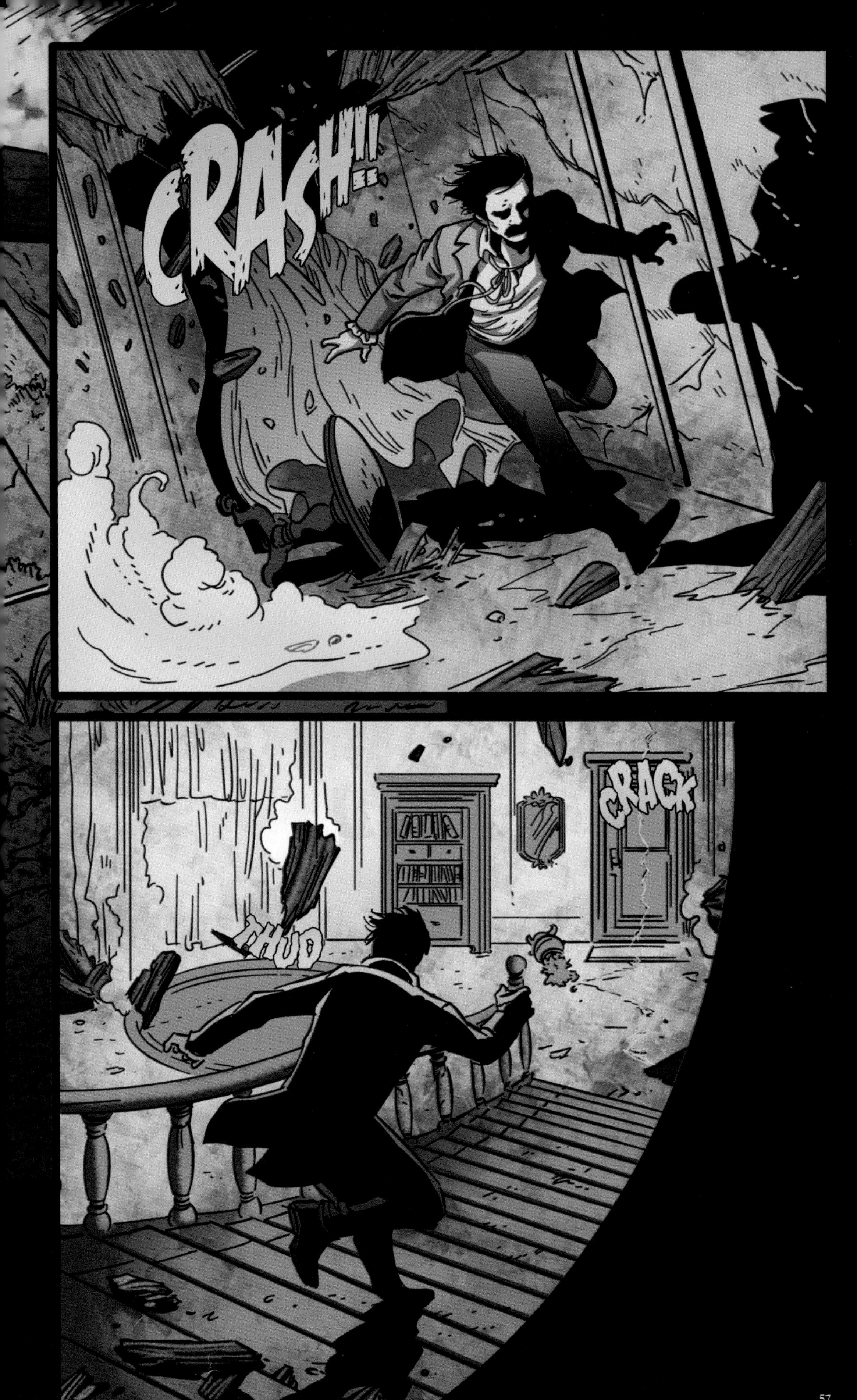
CRASH!!
CRACK
THUD

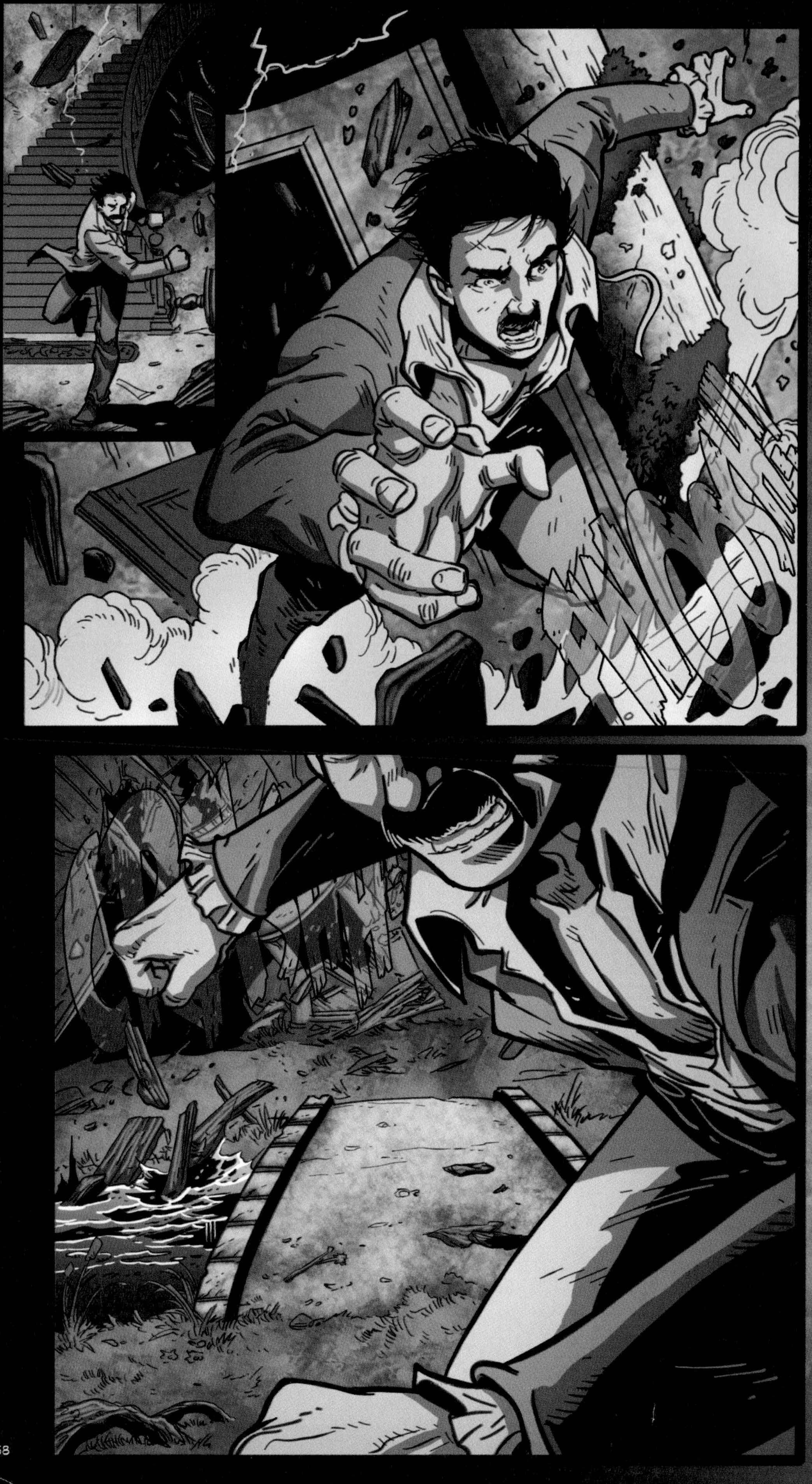

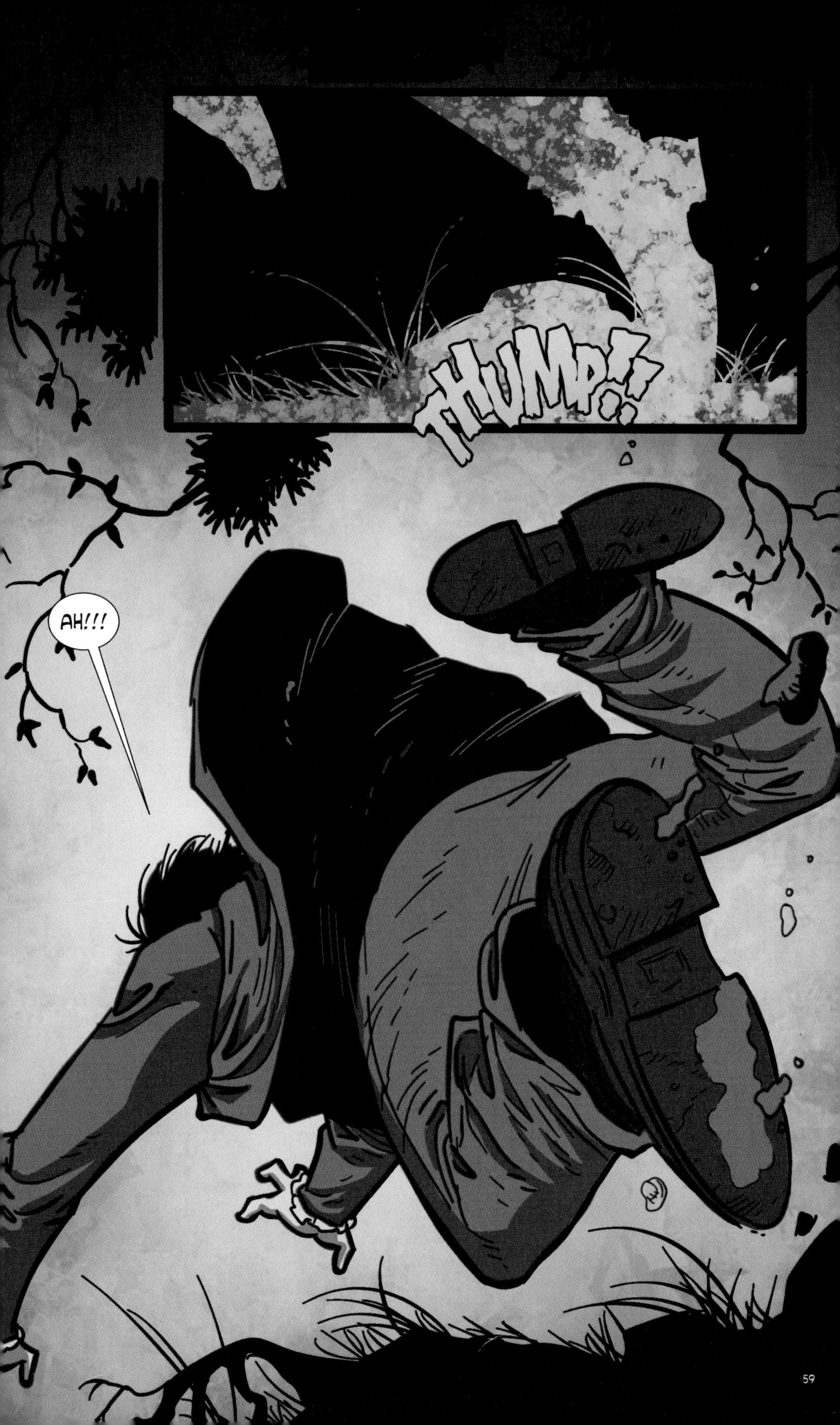
THUMP!!!
AH!!!

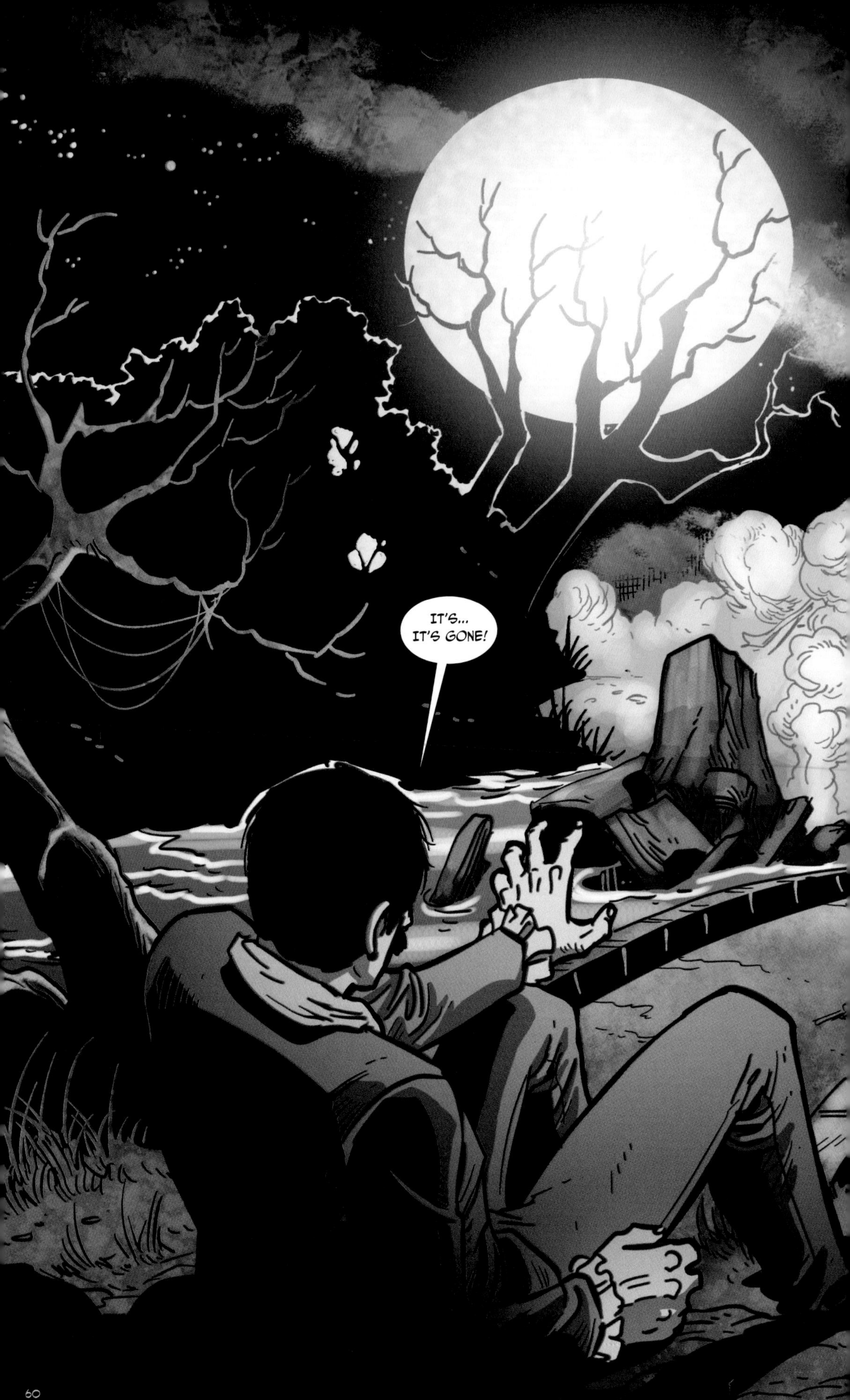
IT'S...
IT'S GONE!

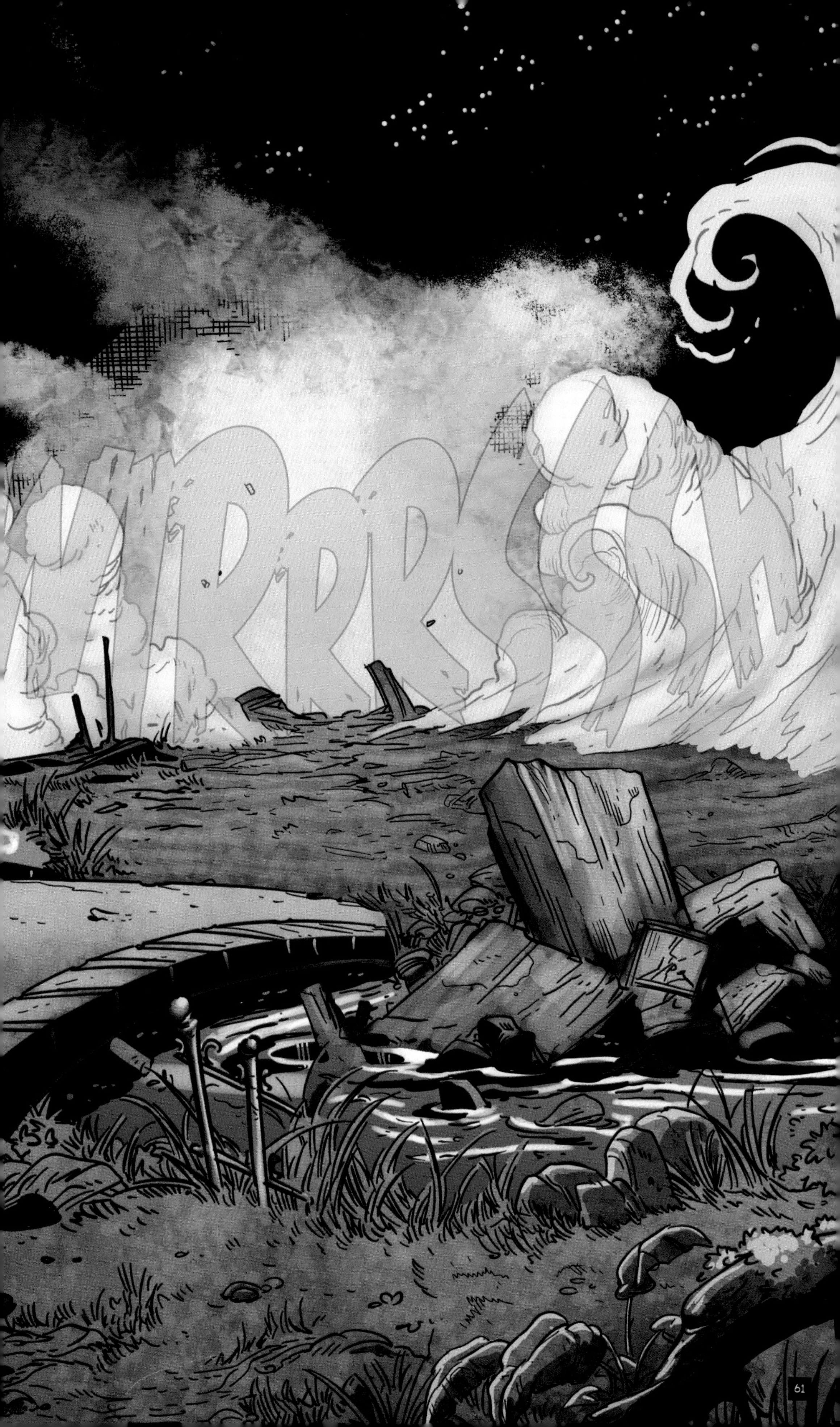
WHRRSSH

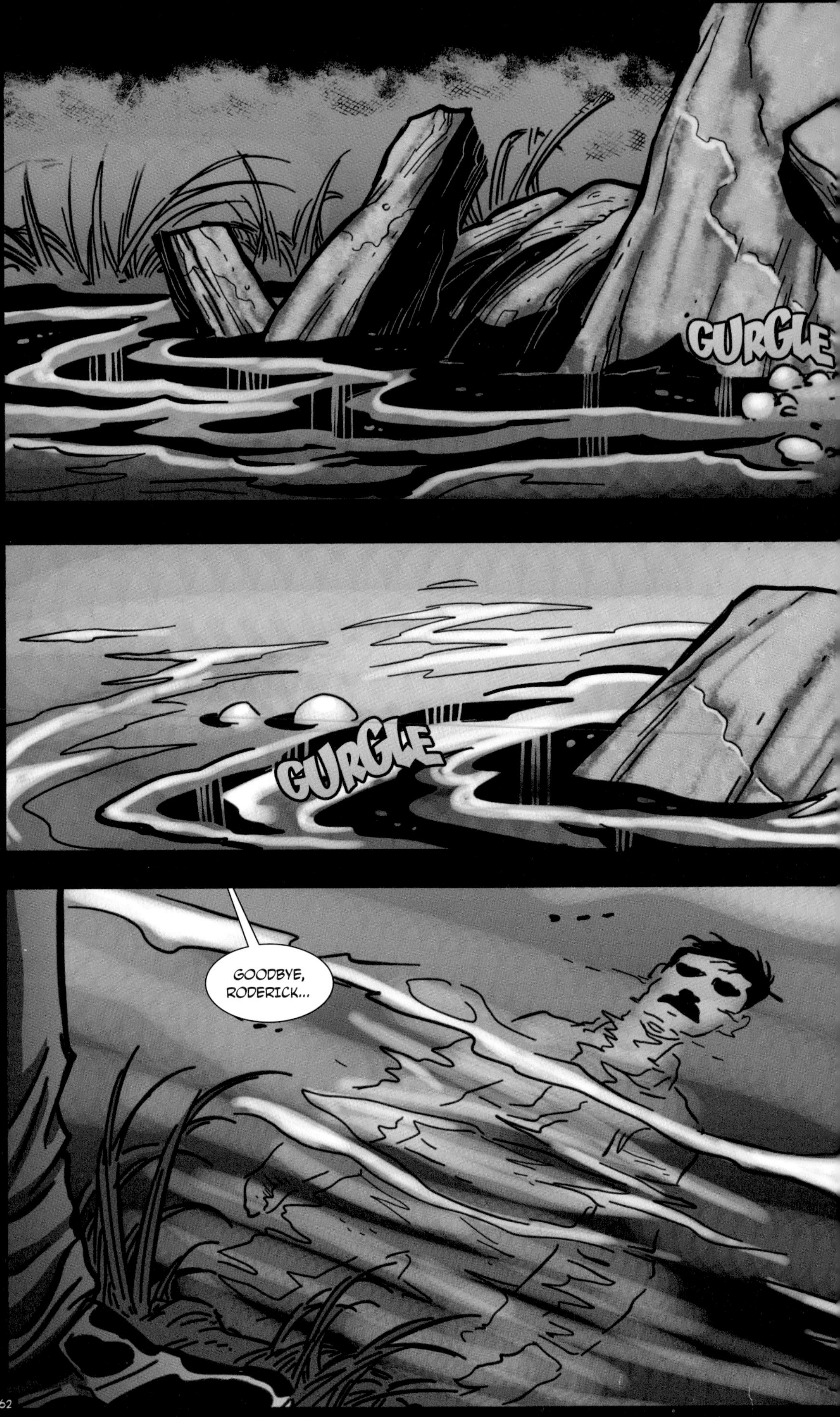
GURGLE
GURGLE
GOODBYE, RODERICK...

GURGLE
MAY THE HOUSE OF USHER REST IN PEACE.

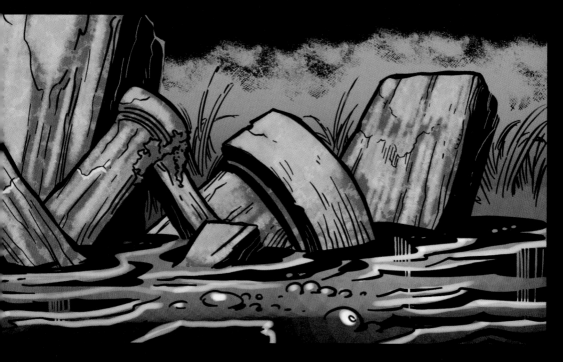

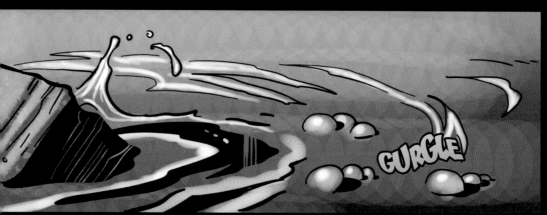

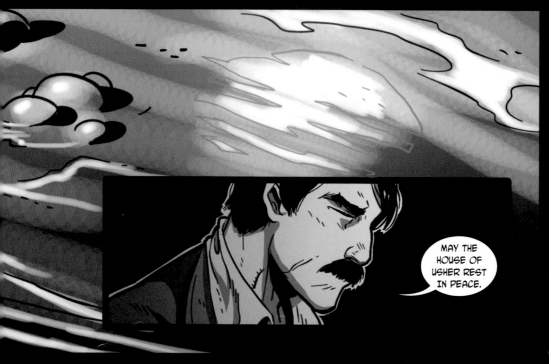

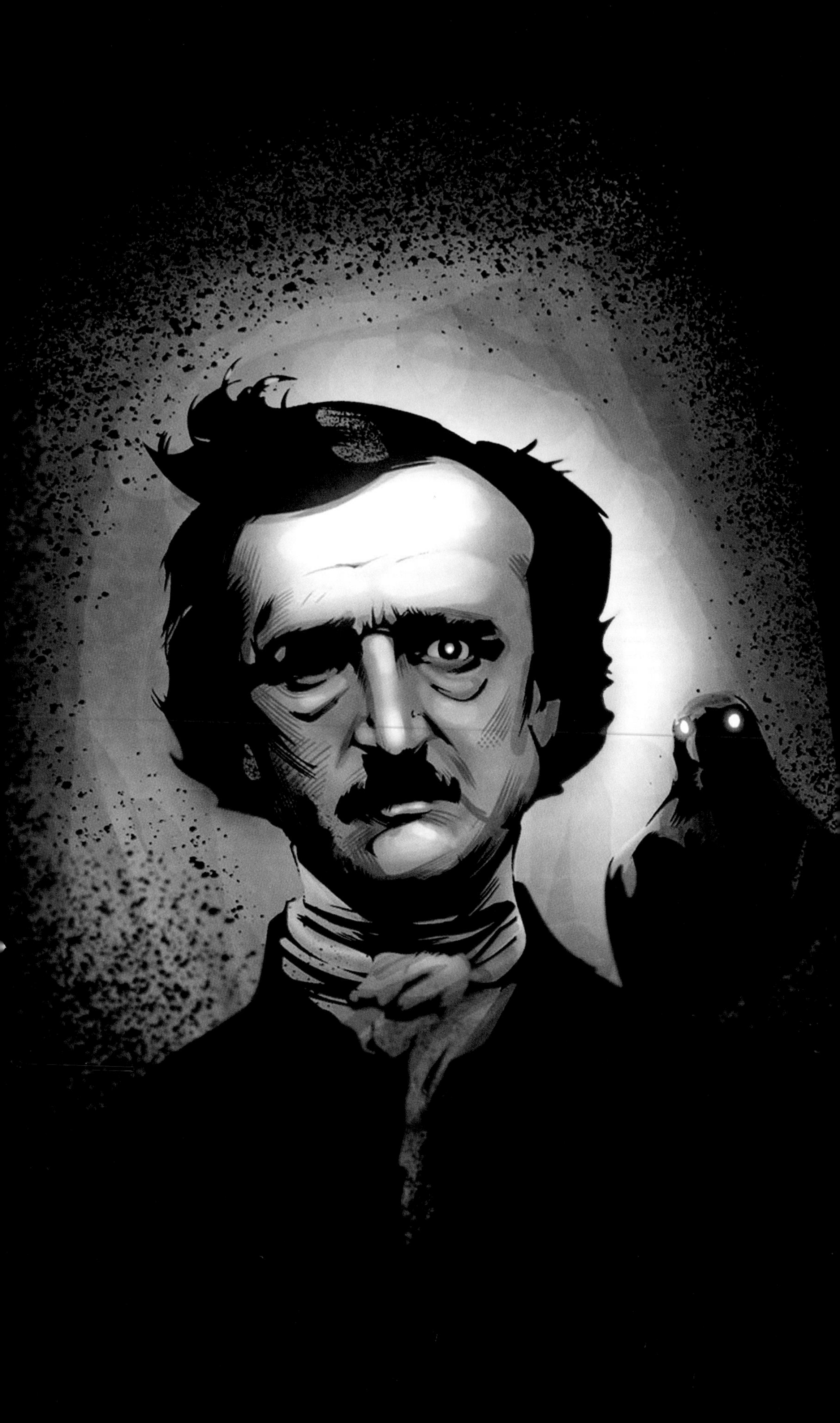

Over the course of his life, Edgar Allan Poe submitted many stories and poems to a number of publications. All of them were either rejected, or he received little to no compensation for them. His most popular work, "The Raven", quite nearly made him a household name--but only earned him nine dollars.

Poe was unable to hold a single job for very long, jumping from position to position for most of his life. He had very few friends, was in constant financial trouble, and struggled with alcoholism throughout his adult years. Edgar's family rarely helped him during these difficult times. In fact, when Edgar's father died in 1834, he did not even mention Edgar in his will.

Though largely unappreciated in his own lifetime, Edgar Allan Poe is now recognized as one of the most important writers of American literature.

THE RETELLING AUTHOR

MATTHEW K. MANNING is a comic book writer, historian, and fan. Over the course of his career, he's written comics or books starring Batman, Superman, Iron Man, Wolverine, Captain America, Thor, Spider-Man, the Incredible Hulk, the Flash, the Legion of Super-Heroes, the Justice League, and even Bugs Bunny. Some of his more recent works include the popular hardcover for Andrews McMeel Publishing entitled *The Batman Files* and an upcoming creator-owned six-issue mini-series for DC Comics. He lives in Mystic, Connecticut with his wife Dorothy and daughter Lillian.

THE ILLUSTRATOR

JIM JIMENZ is in a band with his brothers, Jay and Joy. Together, they have performed as the JBROTHERS for many years now. Jim's been a comic artist even longer, working as an animator and layout artist for Walt Disney and Hanna Barbera.

GLOSSARY

CHAMPION (*CHAM-pee-uhn*)--a fighter or warrior

COMPANIONSHIP (*kuhm-PAN-yuhn-ship*)--the act of keeping a person company, or being a friend to someone

DISCORDANT (*diss-KORD-uhnt*)--harsh sounding, unpleasant to hear, or out of tune

DISTRAUGHT (*di-STRAWT*)--deeply agitated or crazy

DUBIOUS (*DOO-bee-uhss*)--unsure or questionable

DWELLING (*DWEL-ing*)--the place where someone or something lives, such as a house, apartment, cave, etc.

ENTOMB (*en-TOOM*)--to bury or place in a tomb

GRIEVING (*GREE-ving*)--feeling very sad, usually because someone has died

HIDEOUS (*HID-ee-uhss*)--ugly or horrible

INFECTIOUS (*in-FEK-shuhss*)--if something is infectious, it spreads easily

RESEMBLANCE (*ri-ZEM-bluhnss*)--a similarity in appearance or likeness

SENTIENCE (*SEN-shuhnss*)--the capacity for sensation or feeling

VAST (*VAST*)--huge in area or extent

VIGIL (*VIJ-uhl*)--a watch or a period of watchful attention occuring at night or at other times

VISUAL QUESTIONS

1. The Usher family's house affects the people inside it. Identify a few points in this story where the house seems to be influencing its guests.

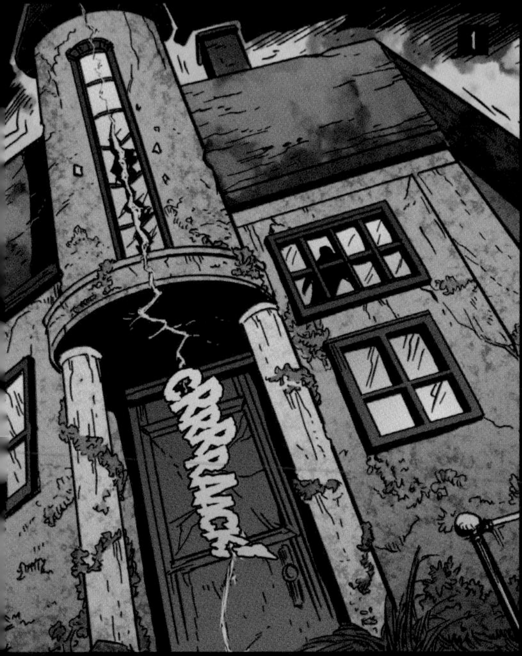
1
CRRRRACK

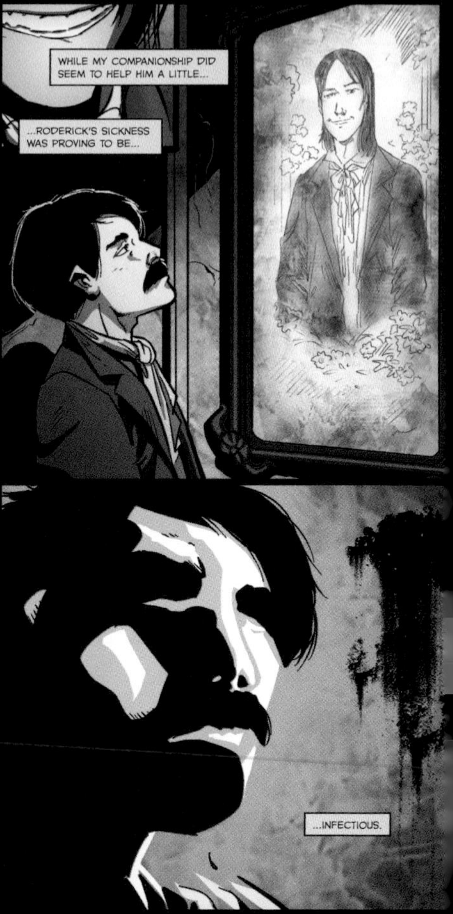
WHILE MY COMPANIONSHIP DID SEEM TO HELP HIM A LITTLE...
...RODERICK'S SICKNESS WAS PROVING TO BE...
...INFECTIOUS.

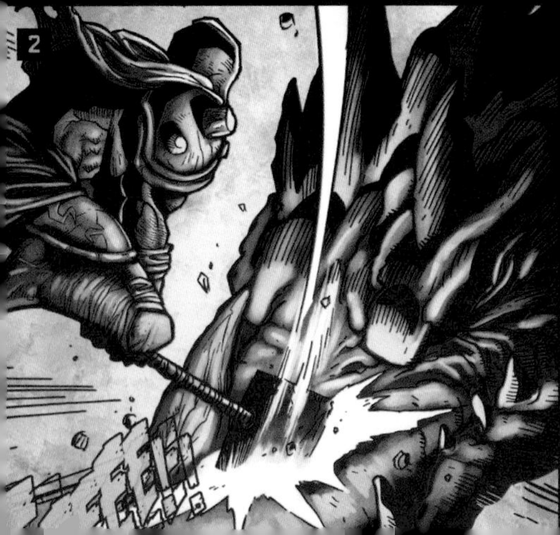
2

2. This book has another story within it, *Mad Trist*, that features a brave knight and a fierce dragon. What does *Mad Trist* have in common with *The Fall of the House of Usher*? Why do you think *Mad Trist* was included in this book? Find a few places in the art where the two stories overlap.

3. Roderick Usher admits that he often thinks about whether or not plants are sentient, or can think. Identify a few points in this story where plants or nature affect the house of Usher or its inhabitants.

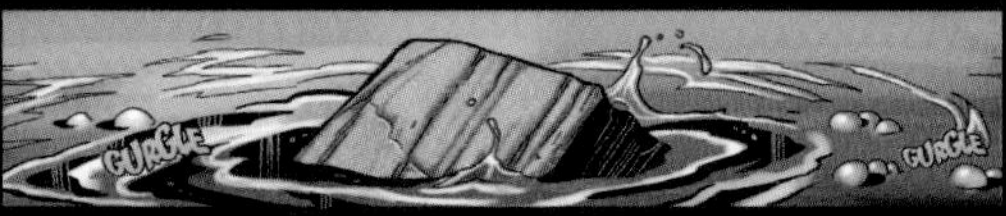
GURGLE
GURGLE

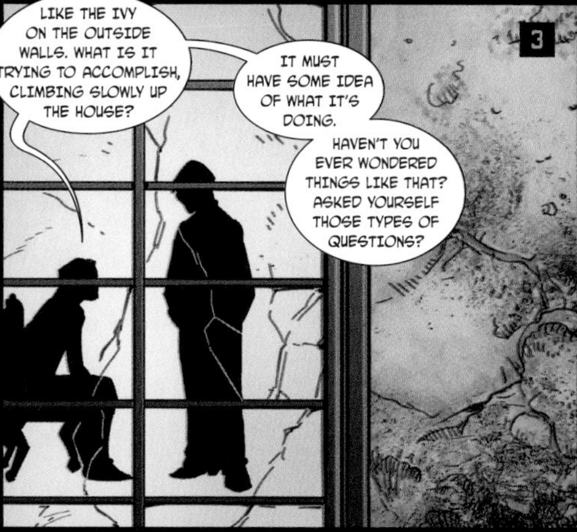
3
LIKE THE IVY ON THE OUTSIDE WALLS. WHAT IS IT TRYING TO ACCOMPLISH, CLIMBING SLOWLY UP THE HOUSE?
IT MUST HAVE SOME IDEA OF WHAT IT'S DOING.
HAVEN'T YOU EVER WONDERED THINGS LIKE THAT? ASKED YOURSELF THOSE TYPES OF QUESTIONS?

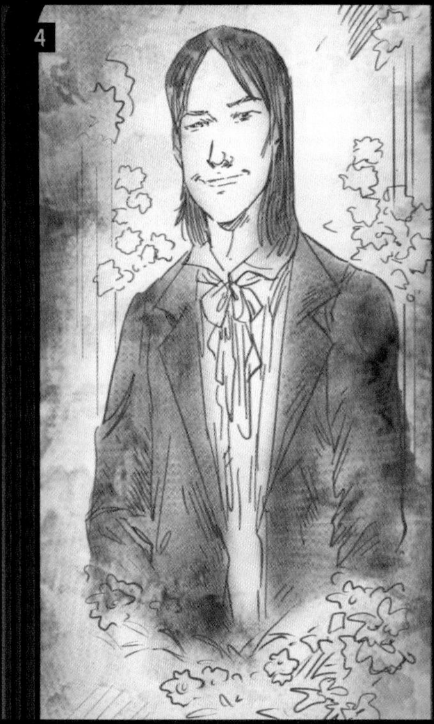
4

4. The name of the short story that inspired this book is called *The Fall of the House of Usher.* Why do you think Poe chose this title? There are a couple ways the "House of Usher" in the title can be defined. Can you figure out two of them?

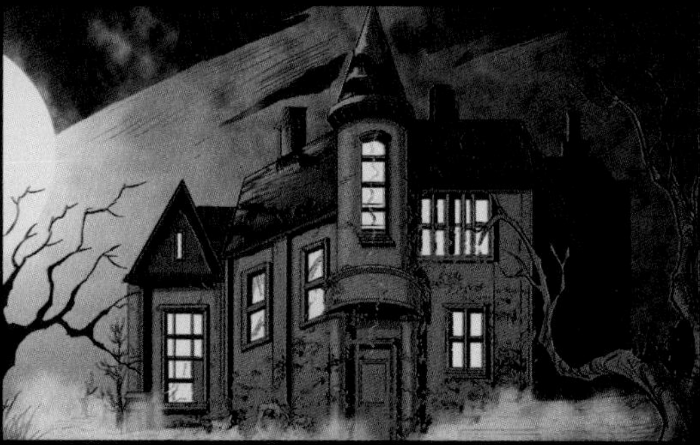

5. Why do you think the house falls down when it does? Explain your answer using examples from the illustrations and the text.

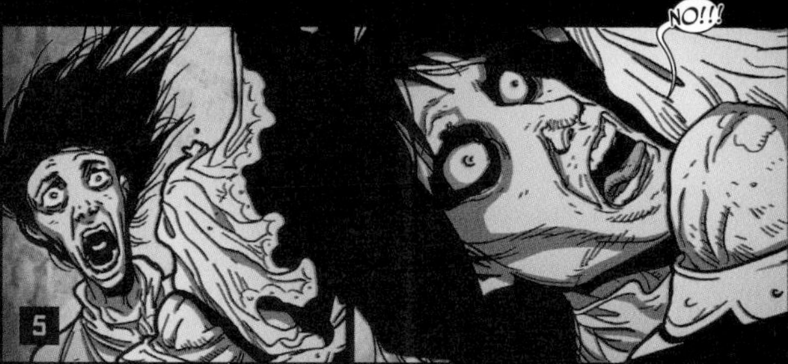
NO!!!
5

INTRODUCING ANOTHER POE GRAPHIC NOVEL...

THE MURDERS IN THE RUE MORGUE

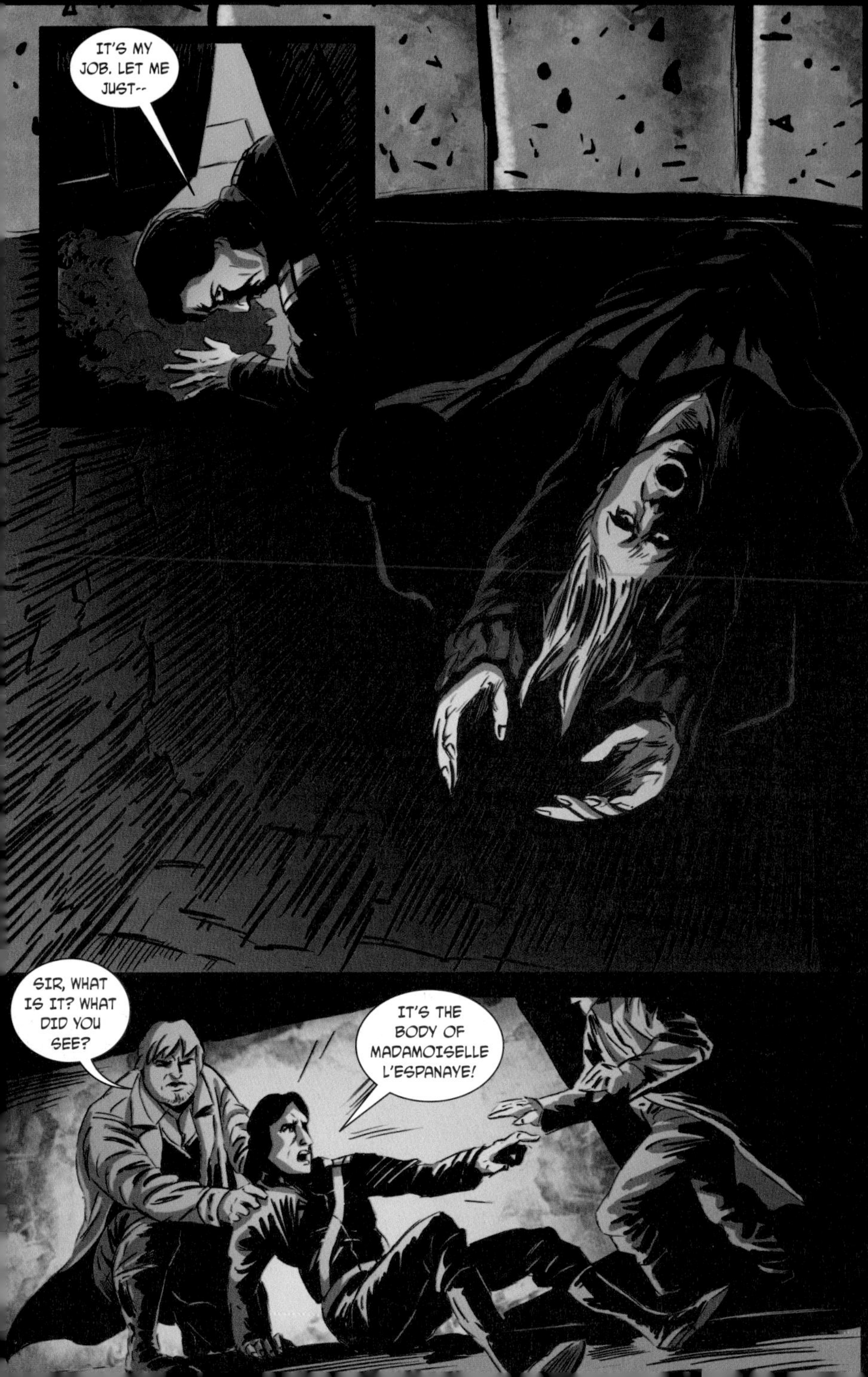
IT'S MY JOB. LET ME JUST--
SIR, WHAT IS IT? WHAT DID YOU SEE?
IT'S THE BODY OF MADAMOISELLE L'ESPANAYE!

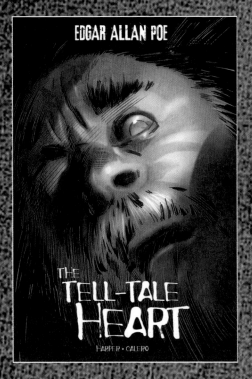

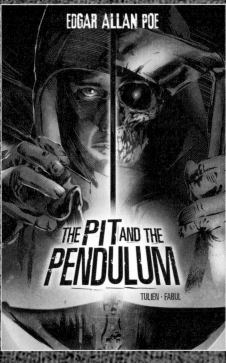
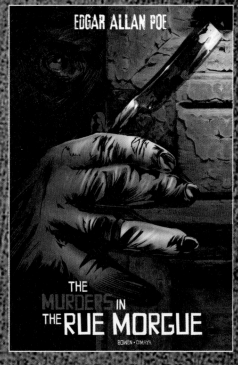

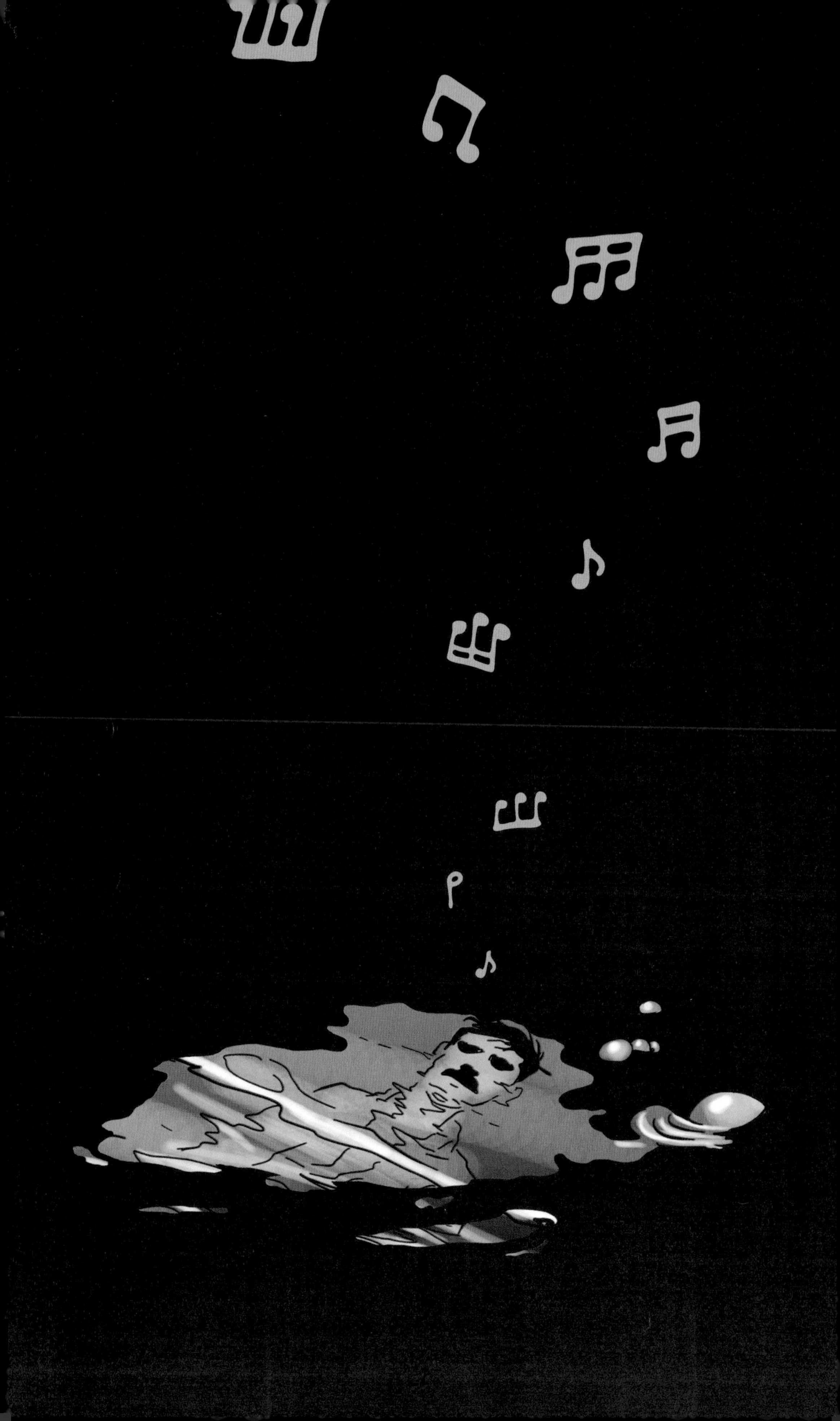